NOT NORMAL

M. G. HIGGINS

SADDLEBACK
PUBLISHING

GRAVEL ROAD

Bi-Normal
Edge of Ready
Falling Out of Place
Screaming Quietly
2 Days
Unchained

SADDLEBACK
PUBLISHING
www.sdlback.com

Copyright ©2013 by Saddleback Educational Publishing
All rights reserved. No part of this book may be reproduced in any form or by any means, electronic or mechanical, including photocopying, recording, scanning, or by any information storage and retrieval system, without the written permission of the publisher. SADDLEBACK EDUCATIONAL PUBLISHING and any associated logos are trademarks and/or registered trademarks of Saddleback Educational Publishing.

ISBN-13: 978-1-62250-004-8
ISBN-10: 1-62250-004-0
eBook: 978-1-61247-688-9

Printed in Guangzhou, China
NOR/0313/CA21300352

17 16 15 14 13   1 2 3 4 5

_S_ometimes we find ourselves on a gravel road, not sure of how we got there or where the road leads. Sharp stones pellet the unprotected. And the everyday wear and tear sears more deeply.

Darla, my twelve-year-old sister, has shoved me halfway off the computer chair. "Brett, move!" she yells.

"Cool it!" I yell back. "I have to finish this essay."

"I have to do my book report." She stops shoving. "Dad! It's my turn at the computer."

Behind me, I hear the clink of cereal bowls landing on the kitchen table. "Why didn't you do your book report last night?" Dad asks.

"Because I was doing other stuff," Darla says.

"Same here," I say. "We need our own computers."

He sighs. Loudly. Opens the fridge. Looks in. Closes it.

I type the last sentence of my essay. Click Print. "Dad, you're too paranoid."

"There *are* online predators," he says. "I want the computer where I can see what you're doing."

I get to my feet and grab the printout. Darla scoots into my place. "Ew, the seat is sweaty."

"It is not." I shove the essay in my notebook. Sit across from Dad at the table. "I wish you'd trust us more."

"I trust you. It's other people I don't trust."

"Yeah, whatever," I mutter, grabbing the cereal box.

"Yeah, whatever," Darla parrots. This is the only subject in the world my sister and I agree on.

I quickly go through a bowl of cereal. Banana. Big glass of orange juice. Football season is over, but I feel like I'm still in training. I pour another bowl of cereal. Grab another banana.

Dad frowns and shakes his head.

"What?" I ask.

"Nothing," he says, staring into his coffee cup.

I return the banana to the fruit bowl.

He grunts. Grabs the banana and tosses it at me. "Eat. You're sixteen."

Man, make up your mind. I shrug and start peeling it. "Not going out today?"

He shakes his head. "Water's too rough."

I look at him. He's still not making eye contact. His shoulders are slumped. Most of the time Dad's able to fish. But when he doesn't, there's no income. He's too proud to talk about money. Doesn't want to worry us. Which just makes me worry.

Money … everything … was so much easier before Mom died.

"Burger King is hiring," I say. "I saw a sign—"

"No," Dad interrupts me. "Your job is school."

I take a deep breath and finish the banana. "It's okay about the computer. We can get by with one."

"No we can't," Darla pipes up.

"Darla, shut up."

Dad's so preoccupied he doesn't even scold me. I know the whole computer thing is more about money than cyber stalkers. Why can't he just say that? *Guys, we can't afford another computer.* Why does he have to be such a super parent?

I get up from the table. Clean my dishes and grab my backpack. "Well, see ya later."

"Yeah. Have a good one." Dad's voice

trails off. Like he's got ten thousand things on his mind. Things I'll never know about.

I'm standing at my locker. Hear, "Hey, Miller." Fermio whacks his forearm against mine. I notice a new bruise on the side of his face. A big one this time. He and his dad must have really gotten into it. A couple other friends from the team— Josh and Keesy—hover next to Fermio.

"Hey." I open my locker.

Josh says, "I saw an old Nissan at Earl's this morning."

"Oh yeah? I'll have to check it out." My 1996 Nissan pickup is too old and beat up to be cool. But it's old and beat up enough to be cheap. Earl's junkyard is my go-to place for spare parts.

I feel fingers tickling my sides.

"Don't look now," Fermio says, grinning and glancing behind me. "It's Jillia the gorillia." The guys laugh and take off.

I twist around. "Hey," I say.

"Hey," Jillia says, all purry and sexy. She wraps her arms around my waist. Her hair smells like apples. I cup her face in my hands and give her a long kiss. Taste her blueberry lip gloss.

"Yum, I want to eat your face."

"I don't think so." She pulls away, wrinkling her nose.

"What?"

"Um, did you brush your teeth this morning?"

I slap my hand over my mouth. "No," I say through my fingers. "Sorry."

She smiles. Digs in her backpack and pulls out a mint. "Here."

I toss the mint in my mouth. "I guess I was distracted."

"About what?"

"Just … stuff. Family stuff."

Her phone chirps, and she snickers as she reads the screen.

"Shannon?" I ask. That's her best friend.

"Yeah." She smirks. "Says she's gonna beat my ass at batting drills today. I don't *think* so." Jillia fingers her keyboard.

"I gotta hike it," I say. "See you at lunch." I kiss Jillia's forehead in case my breath is still gross.

My first class is drawing. Which is in the art building on the other side of campus. I can hardly draw a straight line, but I needed an elective. Guys on the team say Mr. Spencer is cool. An easy A. It's only the third day of the second semester, so too early to tell. I do like the art room. It's so … un-academic. About twenty easels and stools are scattered around in a jumbled semi-circle. Each easel holds a large pad of paper.

It's late when I get to class. I grab the last untaken spot along the side of the room. The bell rings just as I land my butt on the stool.

There's a message in big letters on the whiteboard:

Mr. Spencer will be 30 minutes late.
Continue perspective exercises.

Perspective. Okay. I was kind of focused on a phone-app game yesterday. I glance at the guy next to me. He's drawing a 3-D box. "Oh, right," I say, still not sure.

He looks over at me. Smiles. I've seen him around once or twice but don't really know him. "Horizon line?" he says.

"Uh-huh."

"Vanishing point?"

"Uh-huh."

"Were you even here yesterday?"

"Uh … huh?"

He laughs. Reaches over with his pencil. Draws a line across the top third of my page. "Horizon line," he says. His arm extends close to my nose. A rich, soapy scent wafts over. I suddenly wonder if my breath is still bad. Wish I had another mint. Then wonder why I care.

He puts a dot on the middle of the line. "Vanishing point. Where all three-dimensional objects end?"

"Right. It's coming back to me now."

He smiles again. "I'm Zach."

"Brett," I say. "Thanks for the help."

"No prob." Zach turns back to his easel. I catch his profile as I glance at the boxes he's sketching on his drawing pad. I notice his tanned skin. The outline of his biceps under his tight long-sleeved T. He looks over. I flick my eyes back to my easel. Grip the pencil in my fist. Feel the point dig into my skin. What is wrong with me?

CHAPTER 2

I want to think I don't ask for Zach's help again during class. That when he reaches over to my drawing pad, I don't smell his delicious arm again. That while Mr. Spencer lectures, I don't keep glancing at Zach, imagining what his biceps look like with his shirt off. But I do.

When Mr. Spencer says, "Okay, time to clean up," I'm confused. Like I'm waking up from an hour-long daydream. I sit on my stool, listening to pencils clattering on wooden trays. Paper rustling. Kids chattering. Then the bell rings. Like a slap to my face, the ugly noise jolts me back to reality.

What am I doing?

I jump off of my stool. I have to get out of here. Now. I quickly rip the page from my easel. Crumple it in a ball.

"Hey, didn't you hear?" Zach says. "We're supposed to sign our pages and turn them in."

"No. I didn't hear," I say without looking at him. My face is burning.

"O-kay. See you tomorrow."

I run out of the art building. Throw my drawing in a trash can outside the door. I barrel through the main hallway. I can't get the embarrassed heat out of my face. The jittery, disgusted feeling out of my stomach. I was lusting after a guy! I shove through a crowd of gossiping freshmen.

"Hey!" one of the girls yells at me.

I slam into a kid who's texting.

"Watch it, dude!" he whines.

I reach my locker. Turn my combination. Pull up on the latch. It doesn't open.

I try again. It still doesn't open. "Crap!" I take a deep breath. Press my forehead against the locker. Cool it, I command myself. Just *cool* it. I try my combination again, slower this time. The door opens. I grab a textbook. Slam my locker shut.

By now the hallway is less crowded. The commute between my first and second period classes is way too long. I barely have enough time to get to English.

"Hey, Miller." It's Aguilar, fast-walking next to me. He's on the football team. He's also in my next class.

"Hey, Aggie," I mumble.

"Did you write that essay?" he asks.

My mind is so whacked, it takes me a second to figure out what he's talking about—this morning, the computer, my pushy sister. "Um, yeah."

"I didn't. Not a good way to start the semester, right?"

"Right, I guess not."

Aggie talks. I listen. I'm glad for the distraction. By the time we reach English, I'm feeling a little better. The weird art room is behind me. My English class, with its identical desks in nice, neat rows, calms me. Everything is as it should be. *I'm* as I should be. Whatever happened in art class, that wasn't me. I don't know who that was.

That afternoon, I'm halfway to the softball field. I shove my hands in my hoodie pockets. It's a typical overcast day in Elkhead Beach, Oregon. I see Fermio walking up ahead. "Fermio, wait up!" I yell.

"Going to softball practice?" I ask when I catch up. The bruise on his cheek has broadened out. It's gotta hurt. I won't ask what happened. If he got stung by his drunken dad, he'll just get all pissy. Claim he walked into a door.

"Of course." He smiles. "It's cold today. You know what that means."

"Um, rack-hugging jerseys?"

"Yeah, dude."

"Anyone's rack in particular?" I'm smiling too. Talking about girls is, well, comforting.

"I may have my eye on a certain outfielder."

He must be talking about mega-hot Angela Cornish. "You and every guy in school. And she's a junior."

Fermio shrugs. "I can try." Then he says, "You are so lucky to have the gorillia. Which I completely don't get. You're butt fugly. And totally gay."

I stare at him.

"I mean, what is with your shoes?" he says.

My *shoes?* I look down. He whacks the underside of my nose with his fingers. "Gotcha."

"Fermio, you dickwad!" I can't believe

I fell for that first-grade prank. I slug his shoulder. Hard.

"Hey!" He stops walking and rubs his arm. "Joke, okay? It was just a joke."

"Fine. Whatever." I'm suddenly not in such a great mood.

He grabs my elbow. "Ooh, lookee, lookee." He points toward the bleachers.

We're a few yards from the softball field. At first I don't see what he's so fired up about. Then I notice Nate and Ryan climbing into the stands.

Fermio holds out his fist. I bump it. Game on.

We climb into the metal bleachers. When Ryan sees us, his eyes widen. He turns pale. He taps Nate's forearm. Nate looks up. But instead of turning pale, his jaw clenches when he recognizes us. He sits straighter.

It's just a practice, and the stands are almost empty. But Fermio sits right behind

Nate, me behind Ryan. We don't say or do anything. Just let our hulking presence sink in. Jillia trots onto the field.

"Yo, Jillia!" I scream.

She sees me and waves. Sends me a beaming smile. Man, she's beautiful. Even her ponytail is sexy.

"Dude, your girlfriend is hot," Fermio says. He presses his knee into Nate's back. "Don't you think she's hot? Don't you wish Jillia was your girlfriend?"

I don't think it's possible for Nate to sit any straighter. But his back stiffens like he's got a metal rod for a spine.

"So why are you here?" Fermio asks, his knee still pressed into Nate's back. "Cheering for Coach Ferguson?"

I snort a laugh. Coach Ferguson is bald and potbellied and must be close to a hundred. Though it feels a little like I'm torturing a rabbit, I push my knee into

Ryan. "What about you? You got the hots for Coach Ferguson?"

Ryan twists around. Glares at me. "We happen to like baseball, okay?"

"Except this isn't baseball, dweeb," I say. "It's softball."

"Or maybe you guys don't know the difference between boy sports and girl sports," Fermio says. His eyes widen, and he hits his forehead. "Dude," he says to me. "*That's* what their problem is. They don't know the difference between boys and girls."

"You're the ones with the problem," Ryan says. His face is bright red. "Your pricks are bigger than your brains."

Fermio grabs a handful of Ryan's shirt and yanks him backward. "You stupid faggot."

Next to Ryan, Nate jumps up and faces us. The motion is so sudden, Fermio lets Ryan go. "Come on," Nate says to his friend.

"No!" Ryan scrambles to his feet. He's shaking, balling his hands into fists. "They can't get away with this."

Nate looks Ryan in the eyes. "Don't sink to their level," he says calmly.

Ryan takes a deep breath. Flexes his fingers. Nods. They climb up the steps without looking back.

"Was it something we said?" Fermio calls sadly after them. Then he waves with a limp wrist. "You boys are so sensitive."

Ryan and Nate sit in the opposite corner of the stands, as far from us as they can get.

Fermio laughs. "Excellent." He holds out his hand. I slap it.

I glance out at the field. Jillia is looking back at me. She's frowning, shaking her head. I shrug my shoulders. Then I notice Angela Cornish in center field. She's staring into the stands at Ryan and Nate, a worried look on her face.

CHAPTER

3

There's a familiar smell coming from the oven when I get home. Dad sits at the kitchen table. It's like he never moved from this morning. I set my backpack on the floor. "Tuna noodle?" I ask, heading to the fridge.

"Yeah." Papers are scattered over the table. I take a look as I pour a glass of orange juice. There's a gas bill. Cell bill. His business ledger. Dad's pressing his forehead into his left palm. Twiddling a pencil in his right fingers.

I shove the carton back in the refrigerator. Clear my throat. "So … um … how are things?"

"Things are fine," he says without looking up. His standard answer.

I linger there a second. Wonder if I should push it. Find out how much I should be worrying. But he won't be honest, so why bother? "Okay," I say. "Fine."

I pick up my backpack.

"I've got a fishermen's association meeting tonight. Take the casserole out at five forty-five. And eat with your sister, please."

I take a deep breath. "Sure." I carry the juice to my bedroom. Flop onto my unmade bed. Stare at the Oregon Ducks poster on the wall over my weight set. I miss football. With practices and games, I have no time to think. I don't like thinking, which means I don't like down time. I'd try out for the baseball team, just for something to do during the spring, but I'm a terrible batter. And I don't want Dad putting out more money for another sport.

Plus, Darla's been chirping lately about joining 4-H. I think they have to buy cows and goats and stuff. Knowing Dad, he'll try to make it happen.

Argh! I pound my head with my fist. Enough already. I *hate* thinking. As my mind wanders to homework, it flits by first period—art. Zach. I jump off the bed. Dig my phone out of my backpack and text Jillia. Ask if she wants to come over for dinner and homework. Let out a relieved breath when she texts back, "Yes."

I love Jillia's shoulder. I love how it brushes my arm as she rinses dishes. I know it's crazy, but I'd like this moment to last forever. Me and Jillia, side-by-side, washing dishes. I can imagine us like this twenty years from now. Married. In our own house. I lean down, nuzzle her ear. "You are amazing."

She giggles.

"How do you spell serendipity?" Darla asks.

I glare at my sister. "Do you have to use the computer right this minute?"

"Yes."

"It's okay," Jillia assures me. "S-e-r-e-n-d-i-p-i-t-y," she spells out. "What are you writing?"

"I'm finishing a book report."

"I thought it was due today," I say. "What was all that crap this morning about *having* to use the computer?"

She shrugs. "Don't say *crap*."

I want to strangle her.

The romantic moment killed, Jillia and I quickly finish the dishes. We head to my room. I start to close the door.

"You're not supposed to close the door with a girl in there!" Darla yells from the computer desk. "I'll tell Dad!"

I poke my head into the hallway. "Then I'm never driving you and Larissa

anywhere! And we're just doing homework. So mind your own business."

She doesn't say anything. I close the
door.

"So, what homework are we doing?"
Jillia asks, unzipping her backpack.

I grab her hand and lead her to my bed.
"Sex ed." I pull her on top of me and start
kissing her.

She hesitates at first, then kisses me
back. Her lips are so soft. I move down to
her neck. Her neck is so soft. My hands
are wandering everywhere. To wonderful,
soft places. She's breathing heavily. I love
it when she breathes like that. It's such a
turn on.

"Brett," she pants. She grabs my hand
that's moving toward her breast. "Wait a
sec."

"Let's do it," I murmur into her neck.

She stops breathing. Freezes. "What?
Right now?"

I look up at her face. Her forehead is creased. She does not look happy.

"Um … yeah?"

She shakes her head. Says, "No," in case I didn't get the point.

Talk about a mood killer. I roll onto my back. Let out a heavy sigh.

After a second, she props onto an elbow and stares at me. "What's going on with you?"

"We've been together two years. Don't you think it's time we finally have sex?"

"We're only sixteen."

"So? That's like one hundred sixteen in guy hormone years. Time is running out."

"It is not." She taps my chest with her forefinger. "I want to. Eventually. Just don't pressure me, okay? I'll let you know when I'm ready."

I close my eyes and take a deep breath.

"Yeah. Please do that."

She lightly kisses my lips. I kiss her back.

The next morning I walk into first period well before the bell rings. I stand in the back. See an easel between two students, both girls. I quickly take it.

I recognize one of the girls. She plays in the school band. I smile at her. "Trombone, right?"

She smiles back, her mouth full of braces. "Trumpet."

"Oh, right." As I'm wondering how she can blow a trumpet with all that metal in her mouth, I notice Zach walking in. He heads to an easel on the other side of the room. I lower my eyes.

"That touchdown you made against Frasier in the playoffs was awesome," she says.

"Thanks." I grab a pencil from the tray on the easel. Tap it on my knee. "I guess you saw most of the games."

"Yeah." She smiles at me again.

I glance up. Zach sees me. Smiles and nods. My heart skips. My stupid, idiot heart skips.

I cannot believe this.

I was with Jillia last night. Completely turned on. Ready to have sex. Imagining us washing dishes together for the rest of our lives.

"Hey, did you hear me?" Braces says.

"What?"

"I said my name is Melanie. You don't need to tell me your name. I know you're Brett. Everyone at school knows Brett Miller." Now she's blushing.

Right. "Hi, Melanie."

The late bell rings. For the next fifty-five minutes I'm the ideal student. Focus on drawing like I'm a budding Picasso.

I do not glance at Zach. When my mind starts thinking about Zach, I switch to Jillia. Beautiful, amazing Jillia.

"Turn in your pages and clean up," Mr. Spencer says as class ends. "Remember to sign your work or you won't get credit."

I quickly scribble my name at the bottom of the page. Rip the sheet off the pad. Rush to set it on the assignment table so I can get out of class.

Then I smell him. My knees go rubbery.

"I see you're getting the hang of light sources," Zach says. He's pointing at my drawing. "Nice shading on that sphere."

I don't say anything. I will not say anything.

He sets his page on top of mine. His drawings are amazing. Full of detail. I can't be a jerk. I have to say *some*thing. "Wow. Those are awesome."

He shrugs. "I've had practice."

I meet his brown eyes.

Someone calls, "See you tomorrow, Brett!"

I quickly look away from Zach. Melanie is waving at me, her braces flashing.

I give her a small wave.

"Fan?" Zach asks.

"Football groupie." I roll my eyes.

He laughs. Mimics Melanie's voice when he says, "See you tomorrow, Brett."

"Yeah. See ya." I watch him walk away.

As I'm running to English, I whack my fist against my forehead hard enough so it hurts.

CHAPTER

4

If you're into anything mechanical, Earl's Auto and Marine is like heaven. It's a smorgasbord of used car and boat parts. The place is grimy and a complete wreck. I doubt the floor has ever seen a mop. But as I step inside, the scent of metal and rust and grease is like coming home.

Dad says he took me to Earl's when I was a few days old. Mom never confirmed or denied his claim. She just rolled her eyes and smiled when he said it. But I do remember when I was about four. Running around the bins of valves and camshafts. Shoving my little hands into boxes of bolts. Gaping at the hundreds of chrome hubcaps lining the walls. Amazed by the engine blocks scattered along the floor in the back. They still make me think of metal boulders tossed by ocean waves.

Dad hasn't come with me since I started driving. I thought of asking him this morning. But it's a rare calm day in February. Perfect for crabbing. Dad was up and out of the house at three thirty. We won't see him until late this afternoon.

Along with a few other guys, I'm picking through the discount boxes in the front of the store. A discount at Earl's really means something. The boxes are usually full of useless junk. But I once found some extra lug nuts for my pickup for almost nothing. As I lift out an old wrench, Zach crosses my mind. I don't want to think about him. I've been forcing myself not to think about him. But here I am, wondering if he's into cars. I totally doubt it.

But I imagine us working under the truck together. Reaching for a wrench at the same time. Our hands touching—

I drop the wrench on the floor. Take a deep breath as I pick it up. This can *not* be normal. I glance at the guy rummaging through the box next to mine. Does he ever think about men? And if he does, doesn't that mean he's gay? Because I'm not gay. I like girls. I love girls. I love Jillia.

"Hey, kid."

I twist around. Earl, the store's owner, is grinning at me.

"Hey, Earl," I say.

"Jesus, Mary, and Joseph," he says, looking me up and down. "Don't you ever stop growing? Have the Ducks recruited you yet?"

"No. I'm just a sophomore."

"Well, they will." Earl must be in his fifties or sixties. His Trail Blazer's cap is practically black it's so coated with grease.

"How's your old man?" he asks.

"Okay. Out crabbing."

He nods. Breathes in through his teeth. "Hope he has a good day. It's been a lousy season."

It has? I figured it hasn't been a *good* season the way Dad's stressing over bills. But I wasn't sure. "Yeah," I say, like I know what I'm talking about.

"You guys getting by?"

I bite my lip. Shrug my shoulders.

He quickly says, "Sorry. None of my business. It's just a big topic of conversation around here. This is not a good time to be a fisherman." He claps his hands. "So. You here to see the Nissan I just got in?"

"Yeah."

"I figured you'd be on that truck like a sand fly on seaweed. You know the way." He pats my arm.

Another customer comes up and asks Earl a question.

"Thanks," I tell him and head for the junkyard behind the store. It doesn't take long to find the pickup. It's pretty beat up. Must have been in an accident. But what I really need is an alternator. Lifting the hood, the engine compartment looks clean. The alternator is there. It's probably worth giving it a shot. But I doubt I can afford it on my allowance. I'll have to ask Dad for the money, and I *really* don't want to do that.

I go back inside. Wait by the cash register while Earl rings up a couple of customers.

"What's the verdict?" he asks when he's done.

"How much for the alternator?"

He squints as he looks at the ceiling and then back at me. "For you? Thirty bucks."

It's less than what I'd pay anywhere else. But still more than I have.

"Okay," I tell him. "I'll see what I can do. Thanks." I turn to leave.

"Hey, Brett," he says. When I've turned back around, he says quietly, "I know it's not fair. But lousy fishing is good for my business. People without much money buy on the cheap. I'm busy."

I nod. I noticed there are more people in here than usual.

"I could use another hand. Are you interested?"

"You mean a job?"

"Yeah. Tearing down vehicles. Helping customers. We can work around your school schedule."

I don't know what to say. Working at Earl's would be so cool. Like, I can't imagine a better part-time job. "Um, yeah, I'm interested. I really am. But—"

"No need to decide right now. Talk it over with your pop, okay?"

"Okay, yeah." I shake Earl's hand.

"Thanks for the offer. I really appreciate it."

"You'd be doing me a favor, kid. Say hi to the old man for me."

As I drive home, part of me knows asking Dad about the job is useless. He's just going to say no. But if money is that tight, maybe I can change his mind. It's about three thirty when I pull into the driveway. Dad's not home yet. Jillia and I are going to a party later, so I've got a few hours to kill. When I think about all of that down time, I back the truck out of the driveway and head to the marina.

I can see the radar tower of Dad's boat when I cruise into the parking lot. I trot down the ramp to the dock. Seagulls are swarming around his boat, hoping for scraps. If he's tying up, that means he's already offloaded his catch. His crewmate, Hank, waves when he sees me. "Hey, long time no see!"

"Hi, Hank. Is Dad up there?"

"Yep. Just finishing." He leaps to the dock. "I'm out of here." He winks. "Big date."

I stand next to the boat. Dad's hosing down the deck. About fifty round crab traps are stacked in the aft.

"How did it go?" I call up to him.

He kind of jumps when he sees me. "What's wrong?"

"Nothing. I want to talk to you about something."

He gives me a strange look. Maybe because I haven't been near the boat in months. He grumbles, "Give me a minute."

When he jumps onto the dock, he's gripping a large crab in each hand. They clack their claws open and closed. "Dinner," he says.

I walk next to him toward the parking lot, but not close enough to get pinched.

"I'm going out tonight with Jillia. I don't need dinner."

"Oh," he says.

"So … Earl's offered me a job."

"No," he says right off.

"Dad, hear me out! He's willing to work around my school schedule. It'll give me money for truck parts. For gas—"

"No!" He stops walking and stares at me. "You're just sixteen."

"So? You were only fourteen when you started fishing, right?"

"Yeah, I was. And I wish I'd never gotten sucked into this life. Focus on school, Brett. On football. Follow your dreams—"

"But it's just a part-time job!"

"Listen to me. You would not believe how easily a part-time job becomes a full-time job. Then, suddenly, it's your life." He pulls his right arm back and throws the crab he was holding into the bay. Does the same thing with the other crab.

I let him walk ahead of me as he steams his way down the dock.

CHAPTER

5

After getting nowhere with my dad, I'm in a crappy mood for a party. I almost call Jillia and tell her to forget it. But it's a birthday thing for one of her softball buddies. She'll go even if I don't. And I hate the idea of Jillia going to a party without me. I mean, I trust her and everything. But stuff happens at parties. Especially if there's alcohol around.

I park in front of Jillia's house. The truck's headlights flicker. Stupid alternator. I don't know how much longer it will last. If Dad would just let me take that job. In addition to some income, I'm sure Earl gives his employees a discount. But, whatever. It's not going to happen. I just have to stop thinking about it.

I'm reaching to turn off the ignition when I hear Jillia's front door slam. I look out the passenger window and smile as she trots to the truck. She's wearing her short black skirt. Tight, low-cut top. Her hair is down, all wavy and shiny in the street light. She opens the passenger door.

"Hey," she says.

"Hi. You look really nice."

"Thanks." She leans over and kisses me. It's just a peck. I make it last longer. I'd like to stay parked and make out. But she pushes me away. "Let's go, okay?"

I sigh. "Sure." I put the truck in gear and pull away from the curb. We chat on the way to Carmelita's party. I feel so *normal* around Jillia. So freaking comfortable. You know what? I'm not gay. I think my problem is hormones. I'm sixteen. I think about sex like ninety-nine percent of the time. I've got overflowing testosterone. I so totally believe this is true that I'm in a much better mood when we walk into Carmelita's house.

It's only eight o'clock and the place is already packed. In the kitchen, beverage cans overflow a tub filled with ice. I look for a beer. Don't see any. Oh well. I hand a Coke to Jillia. Take one for myself. Lean against the kitchen counter. Feel the sweet soda fizzle in my mouth. I wrap my arm around my girlfriend. Kiss her cheek.

Life is good. Even without a job, I'll get by. My family will get by. We always do.

"Yo, Brett."

"Yo, Josh," I say.

Josh has just come into the kitchen. He's holding hands with Sanya, another player on the softball team. She squeals when she sees Jillia. They trot off together, all hyper and chatty.

"Girls," I say, shaking my head.

"Yeah. Total mystery, man." Josh picks through the cans in the tub. "No beer? Drag." He grabs a soda and leans against the counter next to me. The kitchen opens up to the rest of the house, so it's a great place to watch the party.

We're talking about my truck and school and stuff when Eliza, the team's catcher, walks in the front door. She's with a girl I've never seen before. Josh nudges my arm. Gestures with his chin at Eliza. "She's totally gay."

"Oh yeah?" I feel my stomach tighten a little at the topic. Then I remind myself this has nothing to do with me.

"You didn't know?" Josh says.

I shake my head.

"Pretty obvious, man. Cropped hair. No makeup. She even walks like a guy."

I watch as Eliza and her friend stroll over and hug Carmelita. I don't really see what he's talking about. But I play along. "Lesbians, huh?"

"Yep. Sanya says a lot of softballers are lesbos."

"Jillia never talks about it."

"Ask her sometime. It's a real eye opener."

I laugh suddenly.

"What?" Josh asks.

I pause. Wonder if I should say what's on my mind. What the hell. "Do you think girls look at football players and talk about how gay we are?"

Josh squints at me like I'm nuts. "Of course not. Sports are a naturally masculine activity. Not so for girls."

I nod, like this makes perfect sense. Take a sip of my Coke, frowning. "So you don't think there are any gay football players?"

He thinks. "Well, some kickers maybe. They can be a little swishy." He laughs and punches my arm. Then he looks at his can of soda. Shakes it. "There has *got* to be alcohol somewhere. I'm gonna scope it out. Wanna come with?"

"No thanks. I'm good."

As I wait for Jillia, I watch everyone, girls and guys. Wonder if they're really who they seem to be. Or if they've got completely different lives going on that no one else knows about. The team's center fielder, Angela Cornish, walks in. She's alone. She is so amazing looking.

"Stop drooling." Jillia's back, reaching her arm around my waist.

"I only have drool for you, baby." I return her hug. "Why didn't Angela bring a date?"

Jillia shrugs. "Probably didn't want the hassle of bringing her girlfriend."

"What?"

Jillia takes a sip of my warm soda. "She's a lesbian."

"Really?"

"Yeah. Really."

"Really?"

Jillia shoves her elbow into my ribs. "Yes. Why is that so hard to believe?"

"I don't know. She's just so—"

"Feminine? Beautiful?"

"Well, um, yeah. I mean, Eliza I can kind of understand."

Jillia stares at me. "You think Eliza is gay?"

"Josh said—"

"Josh doesn't know what he's talking about."

"What about the girl she's with?"

"What about her? She's a *friend*. Eliza's boyfriend is Jeremy Reynolds."

"Oh yeah? He's in my bio class. Wow, and I was thinking half the team was, you know, hitting on each other."

"Yeah, that's not how it is. Personally, I don't really care. I just like playing ball."

"You do?" I wiggle my eyebrows.

"Brett."

"Sorry. Can we go now? I want to make out."

She rolls her eyes. "But the party just started."

"Please?" I kiss her lips. "Pretty please?"

She hesitates, then kisses me back. A nice, long kiss. She sighs. "Okay."

Our make-out session goes great. Until I start thinking about Zach. And he gets stuck in my head. And Jillia wants to know what's wrong. And I can't tell her.

When I drop Jillia off at home, I am not a happy camper.

CHAPTER

6

Sunday sucks. Zach is in my head like a stupid song. I actually go to church with Dad and Darla. Figure a dose of religion might kick this ugly crap out of me. Unfortunately, Pastor Tom's sermon has nothing to do with sex … or sin. I try to listen anyway. He's reading a Bible scripture, and I hate to say this, but it's really boring. I pick up one of those little pencils on the back of the pew in front of me. Poke the dull lead into my palm. Think about art class. Imagine Zach's fingers wrapped around a pencil. Then I imagine his fingers wrapped around something else.

Holy ...

I noisily shove the pencil back in its little holder. Darla gives me the evil eye. I glare back at her. Cross my arms and slouch into the pew. Hope a lightning bolt doesn't strike me. Then hope it does. To put me out of my misery. I'd think about Jillia, but I'm not sure church is the right place for that either. So I half listen to Pastor Tom and imagine replacing the alternator in the pickup. Running football passing routes. The homework I have to finish when I get home.

It's like this for the rest of the day. Zach popping into my head without warning. Me trying to switch my brain to other things. It's exhausting. And it's stressing the hell out of me. This is not overactive hormones. Because it's more than just about sex. I want to *be* with Zach. Spend time with him. Like, go to a movie. Watch a football game. In addition to being cute, he's funny. I *like* him.

It's a crush. I'm crushing on a friggin' guy. That's sick. And I don't know what to do about it. When I think about going to art class in the morning, I break out in a sweat. I want these feelings to go away. At the same time, I don't want them to go away.

Yeah, I could have slept in and gone to school an hour late Monday morning. I thought about it. Right this second, I could turn around and spend first period at McDonald's eating an Egg McMuffin. But here I am, walking to the art building on time. I stand in the doorway of the drawing room. Look inside. The first thing I notice is Zach isn't there. Then I see Melanie, grinning and waving at me. She pats the empty stool next to her.

Fine. Good a place as any.

Taking a deep breath, I straighten my shoulders and stroll in. Like I'm Brett Miller the football star. Like I've got it all under control.

"Hi, Brett," she says as I settle myself onto the stool.

"Hi, Melanie."

Her grin stretches to her ears. She does this wriggly thing on her stool, like she's a puppy that can't sit still. "Did you have a good weekend?" she asks.

"Sure." I search around the room. I think the bell is about to ring. Zach's still not here.

"We're drawing a still life today," Melanie says. "Isn't that cool?"

"Yeah. Cool." What's a still life? I swear, it's like I'm here, but I'm not.

"This seat taken?"

I glance over. My heart speeds up. My throat tightens. "Uh … no," I squeak out.

Recover my normal voice. "Not that I'm aware of."

"Groovy," Zach says.

I realize I'm smiling. I hope it's not a goofy grin, the way Melanie was gawking at me. The thought makes my pits sweat. I force the corners of my mouth down. Shift the easel around, just for something to do. My heart is totally pounding. I look over. Notice he's taking a zippered pouch out of his backpack.

"Chewing tobacco?" I ask.

He snickers. "Nah. I save that for the weekends." He pulls out a couple of expensive-looking pencils.

"Wow," I say. "You bring your own equipment?"

"Yep. Right tool for the right job."

"That's what my dad said. When I tried to change a spark plug with a regular socket."

"I don't know what you're talking about, but ... exactly." He smiles. He's got these dimples in his cheeks.

I clear my throat and stare at the floor. "So you're serious about this art stuff?"

"Pretty much. I want to be an illustrator when I grow up."

"That's awesome. I mean, that you want to grow up and everything."

He laughs. Our eyes meet.

"Uh, gentlemen?"

I look up front. The entire class is quiet. Mr. Spencer is staring at us with his arms crossed. "If I can have your attention, I'd like to start class."

"Sure," Zach and I say at the same time.

My face is hot. I know my cheeks are red. Crap. Crap, crap, crap. Did that look like flirting? Because we weren't flirting. Were we? Was I? I glance quickly around the room. None of my teammates are here.

But they might have friends. A couple kids are eyeing us smugly. Who are they?

I turn away. Try to focus on Mr. Spencer. He's talking about a bowl of fruit on a table. We're supposed to draw the bowl of fruit. It's a *still life*. Okay. I pick up my pencil.

Except I'm sweating like crazy. The pencil slides in my clammy fingers. I can feel sweat running down my sides. I can't breathe. It's so friggin' hot in here. I'm going to puke. Or explode. I set my pencil down. Whisper to Melanie, "Tell Spencer I got sick."

She nods with a worried look.

I grab my backpack and run outside.

"I'm sorry, Mr. Miller." The school secretary peers over her glasses at me. Her forehead is creased with fake sympathy. "It's too late in the semester to transfer. And all elective classes are full."

"Even music appreciation?"

"It's full, Mr. Miller. And even if it wasn't, it's—"

"Too late in the semester," I finish for her. "I get it." I slide my backpack off the counter. "Thanks."

"And next time, don't leave class without a permission slip."

I stomp out. Barely get out of the way of Principal Nakamura, who's strolling in.

"Hey, Brett," he says. "Everything okay?"

"Sure," I grunt back. Being on the football team has its perks. But there are times I'd rather be a generic student, a kid no one recognizes. "I have to get back to class."

"Okay, bud." He slaps my shoulder.

But I don't go back to class. I sneak out to the football bleachers. I'm a pretty good student. I've only skipped a class one other time since I was a freshman. So I feel a little guilty, hiding underneath the stands. But when I think about going back to drawing, my chest tightens up. Like I'm going to suffocate.

I drop my backpack on the ground. Lean against a support post and cross my arms. When I look up, I see gay Nate standing about ten posts away. He's staring back at me.

Nate is not smiling. His arms are crossed, matching mine. I lower my hands, because. … Well, just because I don't want to match him in any way. This is majorly awkward. What Fermio and I did to him and Ryan on Friday was wrong. I admit it. I'm not proud of what we did.

But Nate and his friends are so *out*. It's like they're advertising their gayness. I mean, they even started a school club. Why? They might as well be wearing signs that say, "Hit me, I'm pathetic."

Even so, I don't want to be an ass. So I kind of nod at him. He just looks away.

Fine. Whatever.

But as I stand there, rolling the past twenty minutes through my mind, I'm thinking Nate knows stuff. Stuff I don't know. That maybe I should. Maybe it would help.

I look over. No. No way can I talk to him about Zach. Nate is gazing out at the football field. His arms still crossed, clearly hating my guts. But I can't keep living like this. Not knowing what's going on. Feeling like I'm going crazy.

Am I really this desperate?

Yes. I really am.

I take a deep breath. Look around for anyone else who might be nearby. Walk over, not too close. Just to the post nearest his where I lean back. All casual. Don't want to spook him.

"Hi, Nate," I say.

He looks at me. No smile, no frown, just a blank mask.

"Sorry about the other day," I say.

Nothing.

"So why are you skipping first period?"

His left eye twitches. He gazes out at the field again.

"Okay," I say, giving up. "You're pissed. Whatever." I push myself away from the post. Start to walk away.

"You want to know why I'm skipping first period?" he asks.

I face him.

"Because I happen to share it with two of your football buddies."

That info only takes a second to process. "They're not treating you well?"

"What do you think?" Nate's cheeks are pink.

I know this is advice he probably doesn't want to hear, but I can't help myself. "Then maybe you shouldn't be so obvious."

"Obvious. You mean about being gay? Gee, that would be swell if I knew how."

"Well, you can start by not having a club. Or not joining it. Maybe go out for a sport—"

"A sport." He laughs. "What, instead of drama? Or music? Because sports are so much manlier. And are you saying being bullied is my fault?"

"No. I'm saying maybe you wouldn't get teased so much if—"

"If I wasn't so gay?" He shakes his head. "First of all, I can't be more or less gay. And second, it's not teasing. It's harassment. I *want* to be in math right now, not hiding under the bleachers." He reaches down and picks up his ultra-gay neon-orange backpack. "At least I had a quiet place to chill. Then, just my luck, you come along and harass me some more. Thanks." He starts to leave.

"Hey, wait a minute." How did this conversation get so messed up? "Nate, I didn't come over here to *harass* you."

He faces me. "I don't have to justify my existence to you. You don't know anything about me."

"Um, sensitive much?" I take a deep breath. "Look, I'm sorry. I don't know you. Maybe I should. I just want to ask you something."

His shoulders drop a tiny bit. "What?"

Okay. How do I word this? "I have this friend. He's, like, confused. About … things."

"Things," Nate repeats.

"Yeah. He has feelings for … someone."

Nate is quiet a second. Then says, "Are you saying you have a friend who thinks he's gay but isn't sure?"

"Yeah. Exactly."

Nate nods. Like he gets it. Like he's going to say something meaningful. Then, suddenly, his eyes narrow. He shakes his head. "This is a prank, isn't it?" He quickly looks around the bleachers. "Who's in on this? Fermio? Keesy?"

"What?"

"Are you recording me? You're going to post the video on YouTube? Facebook? Well, you can tell your *friend* to go screw himself." He marches off, throwing his orange backpack over his shoulders.

"That went well," I say to myself. "Let's do it again sometime."

I walk back to where I left my backpack. Stand there a minute, feeling like I want to crawl out of my skin. Scream, "S——t!" Slug my fist into the metal seat above my head. Grab my skinned knuckles. Flex my fingers.

It must be close to the end of the period. I yank my backpack off the ground and head toward English. As I walk past the gym, I hear balls *thwoinging* on the court. Guys yelling. Why didn't I take first-period PE? I wouldn't be in this stupid mess.

I stand in the open doorway, gripping the jamb. Josh is in there. He does a nice layup for a score. They're playing shirts and skins. Josh is shirtless. He's sweating like crazy. I study him, like a girl might study a guy. He's tall. Shoulders a little narrow, but he's got a six-pack stomach. He's really fit. The word *lithe* comes to mind. Like a deer. Like a good pass receiver, which he is.

I admit it, he's good looking. I can see why girls like him. Why Sanya drapes all over him. But I couldn't care less. I can look at Josh and my knees don't buckle.

My stomach doesn't give birth to a hive of bumblebees.

Just Zach does it for me.

Why? I mean, why not Josh? I know every guy is not attracted to every girl, and vice versa. Is it some kind of scent? Tone of voice? What?

And why now, all of a sudden? If I'm into guys, then why wasn't I crushing over someone when I was fifteen? Fourteen? And then I remember. There was a guy. Oh yeah.

There was a guy.

I move away from the open doorway of the gym. Lean my back against the outside wall. The cold cement seeps through my jacket and into my skin. I don't remember his name. But I remember his freckled face and sandy hair. It was summer camp before sixth grade. I was eleven. He was in my cabin. We shared a bunk. Me above, him below.

Jerry. That's right. His name was Jerry.

I was homesick when I first got to camp. He was too. Then we told each other a few jokes, laughed, and got over it. He was really funny. We liked the same things, especially football and cars. We became instant best friends. I remember lying in the bunk at night. Wanting to climb down the ladder. Wanting to get into bed with him. Wanting to hold him. Kiss him.

I cringe at the memory. But the feelings seemed normal at the time. I just wanted to take the relationship further. Get closer to him. What kept me in my own sleeping bag was a bigger sense that something was wrong with me. Boys did not kiss other boys. Boys did not get into bed with other boys. I remember staring at the ceiling, thinking about what would happen if someone caught us. They'd laugh. Call us freaks. Send us home. My parents would be shocked. They might kill me.

Jerry wrote me a couple of letters after camp. I really wanted to write back. I missed him like crazy. But I never did. My feelings scared me too much. I shoved him completely out of my mind. Completely. Until today.

The bell ending first period rings right over my head. I jump, my heart knocking in my chest.

"Are you and Jillia getting married?" Darla asks out of the blue.

The three of us are finishing dinner. I'm scraping the last clump of rice and broiled rockfish onto my fork. "We're sixteen."

"So? Juliet was only thirteen."

"We're not Romeo and Juliet."

"Why are you asking?" Dad says.

Darla slides a chunk of fish around her plate. "Because Larissa's sister is getting married and Larissa is a bridesmaid. She gets to wear a long dress and carry flowers."

"Oh," Dad says. He glances at me, a corner of his mouth turning up. "Not gonna help your sister out?"

"No!" I push my chair back. Carry my plate to the sink. Remember washing dishes with Jillia last week. How nice it was. "Not yet, anyway."

"I want a blue dress, okay?" Darla says. "Not pink."

I roll my eyes. "Yeah, I'll make sure to tell Jillia." I start washing my dishes. "Hey, Dad, um, the alternator in the Nissan is about shot. There's one at Earl's."

"How much?"

I hesitate. "Thirty bucks."

He doesn't say anything. I turn around to make sure he heard me. He's staring at his plate. Tapping the end of his fork on the table. The smile he had a second ago is gone. Now I feel like a complete ass. Even a half smile is rare from him these days, and I just ruined his mood. "Don't worry about it," I say.

"No," he says. "You need it. But maybe not for a couple of weeks."

"Okay. That's fine. Thanks."

"What about my 4-H dues?" Darla asks.

"We'll see," Dad says.

"They have to buy cows and crap," I inform him.

"No we don't!" Then she says, "Well, maybe a chicken."

After doing homework and texting back and forth with Jillia about a hundred times, I finally go to bed. As I try to sleep, I think about Jerry. Think about Zach. Unlike Jerry, Zach won't be out of my life after a week. He's in my class all semester. A class I have to finish if I want to graduate. But just because I've got these feelings doesn't mean I have to act on them. I never

crawled into bed with Jerry. Just like I
don't have to do any of the things I imagine
doing with Zach. I'm the one in control,
not my screwed-up hormones.

I am in control. I repeat it a few times
in my head to make sure it sinks in.

I sleep amazingly well that night. I'm
still feeling pretty good when I walk into
drawing the next day. Like, enough of this
garbage already. I won't let this screw up
my life.

Someone has taken the spot next to
Melanie. Fine. Good, actually. That whole
fan-girl thing was getting on my nerves.
She gives me a sad shrug as I sit at an
easel on the other side of the room. Not
wanting to seem stuck up, I give her a sad
shrug in return.

I don't see Zach. Don't care. I stare
straight ahead. The bowl of fruit is still on
the pedestal. I guess we'll be drawing still
lifes again. That's good, since I missed

class yesterday. Here goes nothing. I pick up a pencil. Flip it around in my hand.

I glance at the doorway just as Zach walks in. He sees me. Smiles. I quickly study the fruit bowl again. Square my shoulders. The easels on either side of me are taken. He passes behind me, his soapy scent wafting over. He stops three easels down. I tap the pencil on the wooden tray. *Tap-tap-tap*. He's probably unzipping his pouch by now. Pulling out his professional drawing pencils. Good for him. Good for him and his pencils. He is a good artist, though. An amazing artist. Now I feel like a jerk for not smiling back at him. I'll talk to him after class. No reason for me to be a jerk. I'm not a jerk.

Drawing a bowl of fruit is harder than it looks. My bowl ends up lopsided. The grapes are weightless bubbles. The apple kind of sinks into everything like a blob.

Mr. Spencer ends class. I sign my page at the bottom. Rip it off the pad. Slowly carry it up to the assignments table.

I glance at Zach's easel. He's still there. Talking to the girl next to him. He's laughing. They're both laughing.

I walk quickly back to my easel. Grab my backpack. Rush outside. My face is hot. My hands are shaking. All the air has gone out of me, like I've been tackled by a three-hundred-pound lineman. Crap. Crap, crap, crap. I cannot possibly be jealous. But that's exactly how this feels.

"Hey, Brett!" I turn. Zach is trotting up behind me.

I stop. Take a deep breath. Wish there was a way to get the red out of my face. I know it's flaming.

"Hey," I say when he catches up.

"You okay? Yesterday the girl with the braces said you got sick."

"Oh. Yeah. I'm better." I press my hand on my stomach. "Cramps. That time of the month." I can't believe I just said that.

He laughs. "Yeah, I hear it's a bummer." Then he says, "Sorry I didn't see your still-life drawing."

"You're lucky. It would have turned you to stone."

"It can't be *that* bad."

"Yeah, pretty much."

He points with his thumb over his shoulder. "Well, I've got gym next."

"English," I say, pointing in the opposite direction.

"Just wanted to say hi. Make sure you're alive and everything." He smiles. That dimple-cheeked, white-toothed, full-lipped smile. "See you tomorrow."

I smile back. "Yep. For sure."

He starts to walk away, then turns. "Hey, I take it from that socket comment last week that you're into cars?"

"Yeah, a bit."

"There's this woman I work with at Coffee Plantation after school. She's got a cherry '65 Mustang, completely restored. You might want to stop by, check it out."

I nod.

He leaves.

I walk to English, thinking, *No way. No way in hell am I meeting you out in the real world.*

For the rest of the week, my new phi-
losophy—the one where I'm in control—
works pretty well. I stop trying to avoid
Zach in art class. I mean, why should I?
He's a nice guy. We're becoming, like,
friends. We talk. Joke about stuff. Tease
each other about drawing. Well, he mostly
teases me, since my artwork sucks. His is
beautiful. Every drawing, every time.

Do I fantasize about him? Yeah. A lot,
unfortunately. The thing is, I don't act on
it. I think about my eleven-year-old self,
snug in my sleeping bag, only *thinking*
about Jerry. That's the way it needs to be.

A semester is longer than a week, but so what?

I can do this.

Friday after school, I'm in my pickup on my way home. Since Jillia and I are both broke, she's coming over tonight instead of going out. We'll watch TV, maybe do a little homework. It's been days since we had a good make-out session. I hope Darla's got a sleepover at a friend's house or something. Maybe Dad will take pity on me and go to bed early. Jillia hasn't told me sex is a *go* yet, but I can use my studly charms, try to convince her.

I've just reached downtown. Zach told me he works after school today. I'm not much of a coffee drinker, but I know Coffee Plantation. It's the best coffee shop in town, or so I've heard. I've only been there once. It's popular with brainiacs and artsy-fartsy types. The guys on the football team prefer fast-food drive-throughs and the 7-Eleven.

I stop at the signal on Main and Fifth. Straight is home. Coffee Plantation is left.

I tap my fingers on the steering wheel. The afternoon is cold and overcast. Something hot would go down pretty good right now. I'm not all that into Mustangs, but I like restored cars. The light turns green. What the hell. I turn left. Park down the street.

When I walk in, soft jazz is playing over the sound system. Glass light fixtures hang above natural wood tables. A few people are hunched over their computers. I don't recognize anyone. They're all older. It feels like I'm in a foreign country. I think about turning around and leaving.

"Hey, Brett!" Zach beams at me from behind the counter. My heart does that fluttery thing that I hate. He goes back to helping a customer.

I take my time walking up to the counter. Study the menu hanging on the back wall. Can't make sense of it. Take a deep breath. My heart's beating kind of fast. Zach finishes with his customer. Comes over.

"Hey. Great to see you," he says.

"Yeah."

"So what do you want?"

"Um … I'm not sure."

"Not a coffee drinker?"

"Not much. Guess I'll have a mocha."

"Whipped?"

"What?"

"Do you want whipped cream on top of your mocha?"

"Oh. Yeah, sure."

He grins. "Man, you really are a novice."

I roll my eyes. "There's got to be something I'm better at than you."

He scribbles on a coffee cup with a pen. Slides it down the counter where a woman is operating a machine that's hissing loudly. Then he says, "Well, there's that game with the pointy brown ball and guys running into each other."

"Oh yeah. Maybe I am better at football."

Zach laughs. "It's not too busy. I'll bring your coffee out. Sit wherever you want."

I find a table in the corner. Fold my hands on the table. Drop them onto my lap. Wipe my sweaty palms on my jeans. Why am I here? I shouldn't be here. This is not a good idea. This is not art class. This is the real world. I'm feeling out of control. Like I'm eleven, up on that top bunk, unzipping my sleeping bag, getting ready to …

No. No way.

I'm just getting to my feet to leave when Zach arrives with my coffee. "Sorry that took a while." He sits across from me. "I've got a ten-minute break."

Okay, I can't leave now. I pull my chair back to the table. Hold the cup in both hands. It's hot. I take a sip. Wipe whipped cream off my nose. "This is good," I tell him.

"Yeah, Sarah makes a good mocha."

He's pressing his hands on top of the table. He's got long, graceful fingers. I don't know what artist's hands are supposed to look like, but they must look like Zach's. My fingers are only inches from his. I want to reach out. Press my hand on the back of his. Wrap my fingers around his palm.

"The car's out back," he says.

I look up. "What?"

"Sarah's Mustang? I can't be gone from the counter too long."

"Oh, right." I jump up. I'm such an idiot. My hand shakes as I hold my cup, almost spilling the coffee.

As he leads me to a back door, I try not to stare at his butt. We emerge into a small employee parking lot. You can't miss the car. It's bright fire-engine red.

"I don't know too much about cars," Zach says, pulling a key from his pocket. "I just know what I like. And this I like." He unlocks the driver's-side door. Points to the passenger side. "Hop in. Sarah's okay with interior tours as long as we don't spill anything."

I want to get in there with him. I really want to. But the seats are too close together. The parking lot is too private. I back away. Almost trip over my feet. The drink sloshes. "You know what? I, uh, just remembered. I need to get home. I have to babysit my little sister. I totally forgot." Darla hasn't needed a babysitter since she turned twelve.

"I didn't know you had a sister."

"Yeah. She's a brat. But somebody has to watch her."

"I hear you. I've got a younger brother. He's a brat too. Maybe we can hook them up sometime."

"Yeah. Hah. So … thanks for the mocha and everything. I'll take a rain check on the car tour if that's okay."

"Sure." His eyes narrow. "Are you feeling all right?"

"Yeah. Great. I just need to get home or my dad will kill me."

"Okay. Well, have a good weekend."

I stroll around the building. When I'm out of sight, I run up the street to my truck. Throw the mostly full cup in the gutter. Turn the key in the ignition. The engine sputters and stalls. "Come on!" I pound my fist on the dashboard. Turn the key again. The Nissan rasps to life. I lean my forehead against the steering wheel. Knock my head against it a few times. Then I push myself upright and drive home.

CHAPTER

10

Before Jillia comes over, I'm thinking about Jekyll and Hyde. The dude who's got two personalities—a normal guy and a monster guy. Because here I am, totally wanting to see Jillia. Thinking about running my fingers through her apple-scented hair. Kissing her luscious, soft lips. Touching her athletically tight, yet womanly soft body.

But if that's me, then who was that guy this afternoon all fluttery over Zach? That guy can't be me. It's impossible.

I get up from my desk. Look down the hallway. Hear one of those pawnshop reality shows. Which means Dad must be in front of the TV. I hope Darla's in her room. Dad glances at me as I walk to the kitchen. "We just ate," he says.

"I'm not getting food. I need to use the computer."

Pause. "What are you working on?"

"History report."

He nods his approval, then sets his eyes back on the TV.

I reach the kitchen. Awesome, Darla's not here. I sit in front of the computer. Press the space bar. The screen lights up. I open the browser. Slide the mouse to the search-engine box. The cursor blinks, waiting. My hands freeze over the keyboard. Wonder where to start.

Guys who like guys and also like girls.

Man crushes.

I love my girlfriend but I'm overly attracted to a guy in my art class.

I slouch. Comb my fingers through my hair. It doesn't matter what I type. I just need to start somewhere. I sit up straight. Type, *Guys who like—*

"Are you gonna be long?"

I jump. Darla's standing inches from my shoulder. "Don't sneak up on me like that!"

"Why are you so nervous?"

I don't answer. Quickly backspace over the characters I just typed.

"What are you searching for?" she asks.

"None of your business."

"You're jumpy and your neck is red. It must be something erotic."

I stare at her. "Do you even know what that means?"

She shrugs. "Something about sex."

I get up and back away from the computer. "I'm finished. It's all yours."

"Thanks." She settles onto the chair

like a princess. "You know Dad checks the search-engine history, right?"

"Yeah," I lie. "Of course I know."

I can't believe Dad is that paranoid. Wait, yes I can. I'm suddenly grateful Darla interrupted me.

The doorbell rings.

"I got it!" I yell, running for the door. I fling it open. Jillia is standing on the porch like an angel. I throw my arms around her. Whisper in her hair, "I am so glad you're here."

She giggles. Hugs me back. Squirms under my maybe-too-tight embrace. "Can I come in, please?"

I reluctantly release her. Close the door behind her. Take her by the hand and lead her down the hall. "We're doing home-work," I inform my dad as we pass the living room.

"Hi, Mr. Miller." Jillia gives him a small wave.

"Hi, Jillia." Dad looks at me. "Door open."

"I know."

We get to my room, and I press my hands against her cheeks. Press my lips against hers. I am hungry for her. Starving. Like she's a juicy burger and I haven't eaten in a month. She kisses me back. Moans a little. Ooh, a good sign. We move to the edge of the bed and sit. We're both breathing heavy. I whisper, "We've probably got fifteen minutes before Dad checks on us. Or Darla decides to be a pest."

She smiles. "Okay."

Holy moly. I am so turned on. After what must be the quickest fifteen minutes of my life, Jillia pushes me away. "Hey. We'd better stop."

"No," I murmur, going in for another kiss.

"Really," she says. "Your dad."

That kills it. I take a deep breath. "Yeah. Okay." I let everything go except her hand, which I grip like it's an anchor. "That was nice."

She nods. Slides down to the floor. Reaches over and drags her backpack in front of her. "Want to review for our bio test?"

"No. But okay." I stare at the top of her shiny, apple-scented head. "So ... are you any readier than you were last week?"

She tilts her head back and looks up at me. "Brett."

"Sorry! I was just thinking that after Dad and Darla go to bed, I could sneak you back in the house—"

"No! I told you I'd let you know."

I sigh. "Okay."

Dad appears in the doorway. "Hey," he says. His eyes scan the room.

"Hey, Dad. Big bio test on Monday."

He nods. "Study hard." Then he's gone.

"I like your dad." She pulls her biology textbook out of her backpack. "I think it's cool he checks on you."

"No, it's decidedly uncool." I get off the bed and grab my textbook from the desk.

"He's just being a good parent," she says.

"He's being a prison guard." I plop back onto the bed on my stomach. "He even checks the Internet history on the computer."

Jillia shrugs. "So? If you don't have anything to hide, why does that bother you?"

"I don't have anything to hide," I say quickly. "It's an invasion of privacy. Like if he snuck into my room and snooped through my drawers."

"I guess I see your point." She looks up at me. Squints. "Wait. Are you one of those weirdos leading a secret life on the Internet?"

"No! Of course not."

She flips through her textbook and stops on a page. "So ... symbiosis," she reads. " 'Two different organisms living for mutual benefit.' "

This is when I'd normally say in a smarmy voice, "Yeah, you and me, baby."

But I'm not in the mood to joke around. I'm thinking about being a weirdo, leading a secret life. And what will happen if Jillia ever finds out. I simply ask, "What page are you on?"

CHAPTER 11

Jillia has family stuff the rest of the weekend. That means I'm on my own. While eating breakfast Saturday morning, I think about texting Fermio. Maybe Josh and Keesy. Find out what they're up to. Maybe hang out tonight. But, I don't know. As I pour another bowl of cereal, I get that image of Nate hiding under the bleachers. He's not my favorite person in the world. But he should have the right to sit in class without being tormented. Same as he should be able to watch a softball game in peace.

I mean, it's not like the football team

hulks through the hallways, stuffing freshmen in trash cans. Well, maybe a couple of freshmen. But we do act like we're better than everyone else. We're stars. School heroes. We get away with stuff other students don't. I used to like that. Now I'm not so sure.

Still, they're my friends. My only friends. I've known them forever.

I drop my bowl in the sink. Decide to wash it later. Dad's out crabbing. Darla's at a 4-H meeting at an actual farm. I hope she doesn't come home with a loaner goat or something. I wish I had a job to go to right now. Or football practice. Even being on the boat with Dad would be better than sitting at home with my stupid thoughts.

Man, I think too much.

I need to do something. Get out of the house.

I march to my room. Tie on my running shoes. Jog down the street. Up the street. Block after block. After a while I'm not paying attention to where I'm running. I'm just breathing. Placing one foot in front of the other. Most of the time I'm blissfully not thinking.

Then, a block from home, I suddenly get a flash why I'm *really* not calling the guys. It's because I'm scared. What if I slip up and say something about Zach? Or what if their gaydar picks up something new and different about me? I know that's crazy. I wouldn't mention Zach. And I'm pretty sure I'm not acting any differently.

But I don't want to risk it. It's the same as if Jillia ever finds out. The outcome makes me want to kill myself.

Monday morning, I try to be cool to Zach. If I can squash my feelings for him, then I've got nothing to worry about with Jillia or the guys. Zach is friendly as usual.

Delicious as usual. It makes me want to rip my hair out. Stab myself with my friggin' drawing pencil. But I make it through class.

As I'm walking down the hallway to English, I see a large, bright blue flyer stapled to a school bulletin board.

Elkhead High School
Gay-Straight Alliance (GSA)
Support for those in the
LGBTQ community.
If you're gay, straight, or questioning,
come check us out.
We meet every Wednesday at 3:00,
Room 124.

They've *got* to be kidding. It's one thing to have a club. But do they have to advertise? I'm tempted to rip the flyer off the board.

"What is it?" Aggie is standing next to me.

"Read it. Stupid gay club."

He takes a minute to read the flyer. Shrugs his shoulders.

"It doesn't bother you?" I ask.

"No. Should it?"

I turn away from the board. Aggie walks with me toward English. I wish he wouldn't. I'm in a bad mood and don't feel like talking.

"My brother is gay," he says. "I kind of get why they need a club."

I don't respond.

"Haven't you ever been bullied?" Aggie asks.

I think about it. "No."

"Lucky you. It bites." He says it like he's pissed at me. Why?

We've reached English. I go to my seat. Consider *Miguel Aguilar*. To me, Aggie's just a good lineman. Maybe he was bullied when he was younger for being Mexican or whatever. I don't know. It's not my problem.

Great, now I'm in an even crappier mood.

I toss my textbook on the desk. It lands with a loud *thwack*. Kids turn and look at me. "What?" I growl.

Ms. Littlefield starts class. I watch as she writes something on the whiteboard. Her hair is short. From the back, she looks kind of like a guy. Josh would say she's gay. Is she? How can you tell? Do I look gay? Does Zach? Is he? Is he just being friendly? Or has he been flirting? Have I been flirting? I don't know. I DON'T KNOW. I scribble back and forth with my pen on my notebook until the lines form a dark blue blob and the paper rips.

I press my forehead in my hands. I'm guessing the gay club sponsor must be a gay teacher. Room 124. Wait. That's my history class. Ms. Tierney? I like her. She's cool. I'd heard a rumor she was gay, but I didn't believe it. Maybe she's just gay-friendly. Or Principal Nakamura forced her to sponsor it.

Fourth period, my curiosity is killing me. I get to class early. Ms. Tierney isn't there. Her desk is in the far corner of the classroom. I casually walk behind it. There's a photo in a frame. Of her and another woman. Their arms around each other. Two kids in front of them.

"Hi, Brett."

I twist around. Ms. Tierney is standing behind me holding a mug of coffee. "Can I help you with something?"

"Um. No," I say. "I was just. … It's nothing."

She smiles. "Okay."

As I walk to my desk, all I can think is *No way*.

For the rest of the afternoon my mind races. What if I *am* gay? Could I really handle it? I mean, live like a couple with another guy? Raise kids with him? I get this picture of Zach in my mind, like the photo on Ms. Tierney's desk. Our arms wrapped around each other. A couple of kids in front of us. And I think the image won't stick in my head. It will be so wrong I can't even imagine it.

But I do imagine it. And the picture stays. And it doesn't feel wrong.

It does not. Feel. Wrong.

CHAPTER 12

By the time I leave my last class, my heart is racing. I'm sweating. I feel sick to my stomach. I swear I'm getting the flu, but I know it's stress. I've never been this worried about anything. Even when Mom was diagnosed with cancer. At first I didn't believe it. Two months later she was gone. It happened so fast. But Dad was there, and Grandma stayed with us for a while. We mourned. Then life went on. Except for the huge hole in our family, and Dad shrinking into himself, nothing really changed. I didn't worry too much about the future.

After losing my mom, I feel like I have a lot more at stake. I can't imagine life without my friends. Without Jillia. I can't handle losing anyone else.

I stop at my locker. Try to focus on homework, the books I need to take home. Someone nudges my arm. I turn. Fermio says in a low voice, "Hey, you got a Sharpie?"

It takes me a second to figure out what he's asking for. I rummage through my backpack. Hand him the thick pen. "Return it, okay?"

"Absolutely." He grins. "You might want in on this."

There's something going down. I slam my locker shut and follow him through the hallway. The school clears out quickly at the end of the day. There are only a few stragglers. Up ahead I see Josh and Keesy. Lorimar and Beckland. They're leaning against the wall, like they're just hanging out. The pair of them move apart when we arrive. Between them is one of the gay-club posters.

Fermio uncaps the Sharpie. Scrawls FAGGOTS in huge letters across the bright blue paper.

I feel kind of numb when I see what he's done. I don't snicker like the other guys do. But I don't complain or get mad either. It's just the way it is. It's who we are. We're the guys who write FAGGOTS across gay-club posters.

Fermio eyes me and the others. "Are there more of these around?"

I nod. Point down the hall. "Language arts."

His grin spreads ear to ear. "Let's do it." He nudges my arm. "You okay, bro?"

"Yeah. I'm fine."

The five of them fast-walk down the hall. I hang back a little. Watch as they furtively glance around for teachers or students who might rat on them. Keesy says something. Josh slaps his head. They all laugh. They're almost skipping, they're so hyped up. Fermio turns and waves at me. "Come on, dude!"

We get to the poster I saw earlier near English class. The guys gather around it like they did before, leaning against the wall. Fermio holds the Sharpie out for me. "Your turn."

I hesitate.

"Come on, Miller! We don't have forever. Write something funny."

I uncap the pen. The strong smell shoots up my nose. I shake my head. "Can't think of anything funny." I hand the pen to Josh, who's standing closest to me.

Josh takes the Sharpie. Shrugs. Writes FAGS across the poster.

"Funny enough," Fermio says, snickering. Then he says, "Come on, there must be more of these around."

"I can tell you where all of them are."

It's Nate. He's leaning against the wall on the other side of the hallway. Gripping a staple gun in his hand. He pulls a bunch of posters out from under his arm. "Here," he says, holding them out for us. "It'll save you the trouble of walking around campus."

None of us moves. I can't believe Nate is confronting us. Does he have a death wish?

Fermio breaks the silence. "Okay. Sweet." He steps across the hall. Snatches the posters from Nate's hand. Rips them in half. Reaches out as if to hand them back to Nate. Drops them on the floor. Bright blue rectangles float up and down the hallway.

"Isn't there some other school you and your faggoty friends can go to?" Fermio says.

Nate crosses his arms. "Probably. Except every school has its bullies. We're kind of attached to the ones we have here. We heart you guys."

I laugh. I can't help it.

Fermio eyes me. Then he says, "Come on. Let's go," like we're leaving.

Nate takes a relieved breath. Closes his eyes. He thinks it's over. I know better.

As Fermio takes a step, he reaches out. Grabs one strap of Nate's neon-orange backpack. Nate's eyes widen in shock. "Get away from me!" He slaps at Fermio's hand, tries to pull away.

"Man, this backpack is gay," Fermio says. "What kind of gay stuff do you have in here anyway?"

Now the other guys are joining in. Josh holds one of Nate's flailing arms. Keesy grabs the staple gun. Lorimar and Beckland move behind Nate.

I don't budge. Part of me wants to join in. Be one of the guys. But I'm looking at Nate. At his beet-red face. His determination to hold on to his backpack. Which has just been roughly removed from his shoulders. And is now in Fermio's control on the floor. Josh and Keesy are leaning over the pack too. To see what fun things are in there that they can throw or steal or destroy. Lorimar and Beckland are holding Nate's arms. Fermio reaches for the zipper.

They're all laughing. Saying gross stuff about being gay. Nate's quiet now. He's not struggling much. Just eyeing his backpack with longing. I get a flash of him under the bleachers, skipping class. Not because he wants to, but because he has to. It's sad. It's just so friggin' sad.

I step in. Grab the backpack. Pull it off the floor.

"Hey!" Fermio straightens and stares at me.

I walk over to Nate. Say to Lorimar and Beckland, "Let him go."

"What?" Lorimar grunts. They're the biggest defensive linemen on the team. They could crush me if they wanted to. I don't care.

"Just let him go," I repeat.

They do. I shove the backpack against Nate's chest. Hiss under my breath, "Why do you have to be so *obvious*?"

Our eyes meet. I can tell he's holding back tears. I can also tell he's too scared to say anything. He wraps his arms around the pack and holds it against his stomach.

I turn around and look at my friends. My buddies. "Let's get out of here before we get caught."

Fermio glares at me. "What gives, Miller?"

"Nothing. Let's just go. We're taking too long."

At that moment a classroom door opens down the hall. A teacher walks into the hallway.

Pointing and glaring at Nate, Fermio says, "Not one word."

As one, the five of us walk away. Like we own the place. Like we're the kings of Elkhead High.

CHAPTER 13

Fermio slaps my back when we get to the parking lot. "Good Spidey sense, Miller. I was worried about you for a second. Thought you were turning gay on us or something."

I shake my head.

He backs away, smiling. "Say hi to Jillia the gorillia. I kinda wish you were gay. I'd totally move in on your girlfriend."

"Yeah. Hah."

I unlock the Nissan. Get in. Shut the door. Watch as Josh and Keesy load into Fermio's rusty Chevy pickup. Lorimar and Beckland climb into Mrs. Beckland's

old Buick sedan. None of us have money.
All of our families are barely getting
by. We've known each other since grade
school. They're my friends. One after the
other they peel out of the parking lot.

I sit there a minute. Hold my hand flat
out in front of me. It's shaking. I don't
think I can drive yet. I rub my palms
against my thighs. Take a deep breath.
That really sucked. As I'm thinking about
how much it sucked, I see Ms. Tierney trot
down the school steps. She smiles at a car
that's pulling up. Jumps in. Leans over and
kisses the woman driver. I see a couple of
smaller heads in the back. A dog between
them. They drive away.

What is this, Gay Day or something?
I shake my head. Stick the key in the ignition. Turn it. *Click*. Turn it again. *Click*. I
shake my head in disgust.

S——t! Stupid alternator. I unlatch
the hood. Get out and look in the engine

compartment. Check that the wires are tight. One's a little loose. I hope that's all it is. I so want to go home.

"Dead battery?"

I know without looking it's Nate. I hate that I recognize his voice. "No. Alternator." I straighten.

Nate's unlocking the Honda Civic in the parking space next to mine. He throws his backpack onto the passenger seat. Turns and looks at me. "I guess I should thank you."

I don't say anything. I don't want his thanks. I was eighty percent with my buddies when we were in the hallway. Flipping down the hood support, I let the hood fall with a loud *bam*. Nate jumps. I smile a little.

I walk around to the driver's side to try starting it again.

Nate says, "Hey."

I stop with my hand on the door.

"The other day. Under the bleachers. You were talking about a friend of yours."

I stop breathing. "Yeah."

"That wasn't a prank, was it?"

I hesitate. Don't answer.

"Did your friend find the answers he was looking for?"

"I … I don't know. I haven't talked to him in a while."

"Well. If there's any way I can help."

I glance around the parking lot. It's almost empty. But we're totally out in the open. Exposed.

Do I really want to do this? Now? Yes. I need answers. I look at him. "Can you get in the truck?"

He nods.

Nate listens as I stumble through my *friend's* recent experiences.

When I'm finished, he says, "First of all, I want you to know you can trust me. I won't tell anyone what you've just said.

Second, I'm not an expert. But this subject is important to me. So I know something about it." He pauses. "It sounds like your friend might be bisexual."

I give him a blank look.

Nate says, "That's sexual and romantic feelings for both women and men."

"I thought you could only be gay or straight."

Nate shakes his head. "Or your friend might be questioning his sexual identity. He may be more attracted to guys than girls, but he's still exploring." Then Nate asks, "Do you have a notebook and a pen?"

"Why?"

He rolls his eyes. "We're gonna play hangman. What do you think?"

"Okay, don't be a butthead."

I grab a pen and spiral notebook from my backpack. Hand it to him. He draws a long horizontal line. On the left of the line he writes 100% STRAIGHT. On the other side he writes 100% GAY. Then he says, "Gender and sexuality are on a continuum. No one is a hundred percent gay or a hundred percent straight. People don't fit into neat little boxes. Most people fall on the left. But ..." He draws a circle in the middle of the line. "It sounds like your friend is somewhere around here. In the middle."

I stare at the circle. "He wants to be straight. How does he move to the left?"

Nate taps the pen on the page. "Um. It doesn't really work that way. I mean, some people will argue with this. But sexual orientation is set when you're born. It's not something you can change."

"Well, that bites."

"Why? Your friend is who he is."

"But the church says—"

"Look." His cheeks turn red. "God is all-powerful. He/she knows what he/she is doing. Right?"

The he/she part is stupid, but I say, "Yeah."

"So did God make a mistake with your friend? Why would God create homosexuality if it was wrong or a mistake?"

I think about it. "I don't know. Maybe to test us. To see if we can overcome sin or something."

Nate lowers his eyes. Takes a deep breath. "All I can tell you is I've been attracted to boys for as long as I can remember. This is who I am. Even if I could, I wouldn't try to make myself fit somebody else's version of normal. To me, I'm normal. I'm not a sinner."

He reaches for the door handle. "Any other questions?"

"No," I say quietly.

He opens the door. "Tell your friend there's lots of information online. Search on bisexual." He gets out. Stands still a second. Looks at me. "Your friend is probably really struggling. Tell him to hang in there. He's not alone."

I stare at the steering wheel. "Yeah. I'll tell him. Thanks."

The door slams. I turn the key in the ignition. The engine starts.

As I turn to look over my shoulder and back up, the notebook on the passenger seat glares at me. The chart Nate drew. I press my foot on the brake. Close the notebook and throw it on the floor.

CHAPTER 14

Bisexual. The word stabs at my brain as I drive home. I hate it. Hate the sound of it. The feel of it. I'd heard the term "bi" before but didn't know what it meant. Hadn't cared. Because it had nothing to do with me.

Now, maybe it does.

By the time I'm parking in the driveway at home, I'm remembering more. Things from my past, like Jerry, that I've pushed out of my head. Like sitting in the dentist's office when I was about ten. Reading one of those kid's magazines. There was a men's fashion magazine on a side table. I remember I kept glancing at it, staring at the cover. At the guy model. He was so handsome. I was attracted to him. I wanted to pick it up for a closer look. Flip through the pages and see if there were more pictures of him.

But I didn't. I was afraid what Mom would think. I knew it was wrong. The same way I knew my feelings for Jerry were wrong.

I walk into the kitchen. Darla's sitting at the computer.

"Dad left a message," she says, not looking up.

I pick up the yellow notepad on the kitchen table. Under it is a ten-dollar bill.

I'll be home late. Take Darla to McDonald's.

Darla says, "I forgot to tell Dad I've got a 4-H dinner tonight. Larissa's mom is picking me up at five thirty."

"Okay," I mumble.

"We're eating one of Larissa's hens."

"Ew."

"If you're serious about animal husbandry, you can't get personally attached. They're not pets."

I set down the notepad. "Did you learn that at the farm on Saturday?"

"Yes."

"You mean you could actually raise a chicken and *not* give it a name? And then *eat* it?"

She squirms. "I could try."

I snicker.

"If Larissa can, I can."

"Whatever. You know Dad doesn't have a lot of money. He can't afford animals and feed."

She twists around. "That's not what Dad says."

"Dad doesn't like to admit things."

She sighs. "Yeah. I noticed."

"Good. So don't bug him about buying stuff." On my way to my room, I ask, "How long is this dinner tonight?"

She shrugs. "I think we're supposed to be home by eight."

I stroll to my room. Close the door. Get out my cell phone. Text Jillia. "McDonalds and homework tonight? 5:30ish?"

A few minutes later she texts back, "Sure. See ya. <3"

I take a deep breath. Hug the phone to my chest. "Please be ready," I whisper. "Please, please be ready." I open my nightstand drawer. Reach far in the back. Pull out the mint tin. Open it. The condom Fermio stole from his dad is still there. It smells like peppermint.

The second after Darla leaves at five thirty, I'm jumping in the pickup.

Headed for Jillia's. And I'm thinking, for every guy I've ever thought was hot, there are a bunch more girls I've thought were hotter. Jillia is *it* for me. She's the one. I know it in my heart and brain and body.

I park in front of her house. Run to the door. Knock lightly, like a gentleman. Her mom answers. "Hi, Brett. It's a school night. Have her back by nine."

"Sure, Mrs. Frank." I feel a little guilty. Not because I won't get her home by nine, but if she knew what I was planning. …

Jillia trots past her mom. "Later."

"Nine," her mom repeats. She goes back in the house.

I open the passenger door for Jillia.

"Oh, why thank you, sir," she says.

On the drive to Mickey D's, the steering wheel glistens with sweat from my palms. "It's so hot." I roll down the window.

"Really? I'm freezing." She rubs her arms.

"Oh. Sorry." I roll the window back up.

I pull into the parking lot and rush around to open her door. She's already opened it and is stepping out. I hold it for her like a chauffeur.

"Um, thanks," she says. "Why are you being so polite?"

"You don't like it?"

"It's okay. Just … kind of weird."

We get to the glass door. Now I'm totally self-conscious. I trot in first and hold it open for her. "Is this okay?" I ask.

"Yyyes." She draws the word out. Stares at me.

Ugh.

We sit at a table with our food. I swirl a few french fries in a hill of ketchup. Think about Jillia's body. Wonder if I'll be seeing it naked in a little while. Then I get a stab of panic. What if I don't do it right? What if I can't do it at all? What if my mind wanders?

"Are you going to eat those or just play with them?" Jillia asks.

I flick the fries into my mouth. Ketchup flies across the table and splatters on her shirt.

"Brett!" She dabs at the spot with a napkin.

"Oh no. I'm sorry! Do you want me to get some water or something?"

"No, I'll clean it when I get home." She squints. "Why are you acting so strange?"

I drink a gulp of soda. Tap the cup on the table. "Am I acting strange?"

She tilts her head and stares at me, like, *Duh*.

I take a deep breath. Stare at my cup. Press my thumbnails into the rim. "Dad is out late tonight. Darla's at a 4-H thing. The house is *empty*."

Jillia is quiet. Then she says, "And you're thinking. …"

"Um … yeah."

I glance up at her. She's stopped blotting her shirt. She picks up her burger. Chews. Stares out the window. Sighs.

"Are you mad?" I ask.

"I don't know. I guess it's kind of sweet in a way. I mean, being all super polite and nervous." Then she says quietly, "When's your family getting home?"

"Darla said she'd be back at eight. Dad later, I think."

"So, seven thirty just to be safe. That's about an hour and a half from now." She hasn't finished her dinner. But she crumples everything into a pile on her tray. Starts to scoot out of the booth.

My heart speeds up. I grab her hand.

"Wait," I whisper. "Are you saying you're ready?"

She shrugs.

I jump out of the booth. Dump both of our trays. Open the door for her. Open the truck door for her. Try not to hyperventilate on the drive home.

Holy crap.

CHAPTER

15

It goes good. Great, actually. Awesome. No problems at all. While it's happening, I think Jillia is into it as much as I am. I mean, she never says *no* or *stop*. But then she gets kind of quiet and shy afterward. I keep asking if she's okay. If it hurt or whatever.

"I'm fine," she says.

We're under my covers. She's resting her head against my shoulder. I'm stroking her hair. Having her in my bed, naked, is so perfect. I wish we could stay like this forever. I glance at the clock on my nightstand. "It's seven thirty. We should probably get dressed." I kiss her. "Then do you want to do homework or something?"

She shakes her head. "Maybe you should drive me home."

She lowers her eyes while I get dressed. Then she makes me turn my back while she gets dressed. It's kind of funny. A few minutes ago we couldn't have been more naked with each other. But I can tell she wouldn't like me pointing that out.

She's quiet on the entire drive to her house. I feel crummy. Like I did something wrong. But I can't think what.

"See you tomorrow," I say as she gets out of the truck.

"Yeah. See you tomorrow." She leans over. Gives me a quick peck on the lips and leaves.

I watch her unlock her front door. Walk inside. I'm ready to wave, but she doesn't look back.

As I drive home, part of me is bummed. Wracking my brain. What did I do wrong? But a bigger part of me is totally stoked. I did it! I'm not a virgin anymore. I feel light, like I can float home. Like I can carry the pickup on my shoulders. I turn up the car radio. Pat the steering wheel in time to the music. Wow, that was fantastic. And I was totally with Jillia. My mind wasn't wandering places I didn't want it to go. Places I was afraid it would go. Man, I feel good. Especially after all that crap I went through today.

I'm in control again. Like I will be from now on.

The next morning I hang out at my locker. Fermio walks by. "Where's the gorillia?"

I shrug. "Late, I guess." I text her again. No response. Again.

"Going to the game tonight?"

Oh, right. It's their first league softball game. "Yeah. Absolutely."

"Cool." Then he smirks. "Maybe we'll have some fans to entertain ourselves with."

"Yeah. Maybe." I hope Nate and Ryan don't show up. But if they do, it's their own stupid fault.

By the time I get to first period, the late bell is already ringing. Jillia never did show. Or text. It's not like we get together every morning. Or like we always return texts right away. But I'm worried. I want to see her. We were *intimate* last night. It seems like she'd want to see me. I'm already looking forward to the next time we can hook up.

I take a seat in the back of the art room. Start to look around for Zach. Stop looking. He doesn't mean anything to me. I love Jillia. Jillia. In the middle of the room is a table topped with a stack of books and a glass ball. Another still life? Really? I have the overwhelming urge to be sarcastic. Damn it, Zach. I want him next to me so we can say snarky things and laugh. I let my eyes wander. Find him. He's a couple of easels away on the right. He smiles at me, shakes his head. I smile back. Can't help it.

Mr. Spencer walks in late. "If you've started drawing this still life, please stop. It's for the painting class next period. Sorry about that." A couple of kids groan and rip pages off their easels. "The rest of this week will be portraits." He spends about twenty minutes lecturing us on how to draw faces. Then he says, "Pair up with a partner."

The girl on my right waves at a friend across the room. She quickly gathers her things and moves. I'm about to turn to the kid on my left when Zach slides onto the empty stool. My heart blips.

"Hey, dude," he says smoothly. "Wanna be drawing buddies?"

His voice is deep and seductive. He's being funny. Right? I feel that stupid heat rising to my face. The desire. I should ignore him. Partner with someone else. But I can't be a jerk. Of course I smile and say, "Sure."

"Cool."

I watch as he gets out his pencils. I can't believe this. Last night I was making love to my *girl*friend. And here I am, wanting Zach again. I thought I had this under control.

"Do you want to go first?"

I look up from his long fingers. "What?"

"You draw me or I draw you?"

"Oh. You draw first." Then I say, "I'm hoping we'll run out of time. I'm going to blow at this."

He grins. "You never know. Maybe portraits are your specialty."

"No. I totally don't think so."

He positions his easel where he wants it. Then he says, "Okay. Look over my right shoulder and hold still." I feel him studying my face. He's being clinical about it. I'm his drawing subject. But the attention is excruciating. His right shoulder moves gracefully as he starts drawing. I hear the *scritch-scritch* of his pencil against paper. He's so close to me. So close. I smell his soapy skin. His hair. His clothes. I focus on his perfect ear. His thick black hair. I want to touch it.

"You have nice eyes," he says.

I swallow hard. "What?"

"Yeah. You're nice looking, if you don't mind me saying."

"Uh … no. I guess I don't mind."

Crap. Crap, crap, crap.

He said it like he's stating a fact. Not like he's flirting. But is he? My face is getting hot. My cheeks must be turning red.

"Sorry," he says. "I didn't mean to embarrass you."

Oh no. He noticed. "I guess I'm not all that used to compliments."

He sighs. "Yeah, who is?" Then he says, "Don't talk for a minute. I need to draw your mouth."

My mouth. His mouth.

Argh! I dig my fingernails into my legs.

Jillia. I've got to think about Jillia. I imagine us together last night. That was so beautiful. So perfect. And it hits me. Like a fifty-pound halibut. Like a tackle to my midsection. I *am* bisexual. I am totally bisexual. I am the circle in the middle of that line that Nate drew.

And I don't have a clue what to do about it.

For the rest of first period, I try to blank my mind. With Zach focusing on me so hard, I'm convinced he's seeing inside of me. When he's finished his drawing, "bisexual" will be written across my forehead. He'll laugh. The class will laugh. My friends will find out. My life will be over.

I sit on my stool like a potato.

"Okay, clean up," Mr. Spencer says after what seems like half a day. I'm grateful I won't have to draw Zach. My hand would shake if I did.

"Perfect timing," Zach says. "Just finished."

I take a deep breath and look at his sketchpad. It's just … me. No letters on my forehead.

"Wow. Awesome, as usual," I tell him.

He shrugs. "You're a good subject."

My friggin' face heats up again.

"And I like drawing people," he adds.

"You like drawing period."

He smiles. "This is true."

I pick up my backpack. "Well, I'd better get going."

"Yeah, me too." He starts putting his pencils away. "Hey, Sarah is working afternoons the rest of this week. If you want that rain check on the car tour."

"Oh. Okay." I throw my backpack over my shoulder. "Maybe." And I'm gone.

I will *not* be going to Coffee Plantation this week or any week in the future. I know I told myself that before. But this time I mean it. It's bad enough being so close to him in art class. I can't imagine sitting alone with him in that Mustang. Actually, I *can* imagine it. And that's the problem.

I finally see Jillia at lunch. She's eating in the cafeteria with her softball buddies. When I approach the table, none of the girls smirks or giggles. So I figure she hasn't told them what happened last night. I shouldn't be surprised. I haven't told anyone either. It's not something I want to hide, but it is pretty personal. I lean behind her. Whisper in her ear, "Can I talk to you for a minute?"

The sandwich she's holding freezes midway to her mouth. She sets it down. She slowly gets up from the table. We walk outside to a cedar tree. She leans against it with her arms crossed. Stares at the ground.

"What's wrong?" I ask.

Shrug.

"Jillia, this is nuts. I need to know what's going on."

She meets my eyes. Then she looks across campus. "I think I wasn't ready."

"But at McDonald's you said—"

"I know what I said. So I guess that means it's not your fault."

"It must be my fault. You're treating me like dirt."

She takes a deep breath. Looks at me again. "You've been pressuring me. You've been bugging me nonstop to have sex. I felt like I didn't have a choice, like I needed to just get it over with."

I reach out. Touch her arm. She moves it away.

"I thought you were into it," I say. "I thought you wanted to."

Another shrug. "It's like making out is the only thing we have in common."

I don't know what to say. I finally sputter, "I can't take back what we did last night. And I wouldn't want to."

"Of course you wouldn't! You finally got what you wanted." She pushes away from the tree. "Just leave me alone for a while, okay?"

My heart catches. "Are you breaking up with me?"

"I need time to think." She brushes past me.

I watch her walk back to the cafeteria. I must have stopped breathing because I feel like I'm going to pass out.

The rest of the day goes by in a numb blur. Jillia. The love of my life. She can't break up with me. She can't! She told me to leave her alone for a while. I don't know if I can. And how long is *a while?* Will it bug her if I go to her game? I want to support her. I want to watch her play. So I'm going.

Maybe if she sees me in the stands, she'll realize we have more in common than sex.

I head out to the softball field feeling terrible. Maybe I did pressure her a little. Maybe I was in a hurry. I wanted to have sex because … well, just because I wanted to. But also to prove to myself I could. That I wasn't gay.

I am such a douche.

When I get to the field, both teams are stretching and jogging. Jillia glances up from a knee bend and sees me. Her expression is blank. I don't wave or anything. Just climb up the metal bleachers.

"Hey, Miller!"

It's Fermio. He and Josh are sitting on the top bench. I slide in next to Josh. The stands are more crowded today. More parents. More students. A service club has the snack bar open. Fermio reaches across Josh. Holds a bag of popcorn out for me. I shake my head.

Josh grabs a handful as it passes by. He picks out a kernel. Instead of throwing it in his mouth, he tosses it down the stands. It lands on top of a woman's head. Her hair is so poofed up she doesn't feel it. Josh and Fermio snicker. I wonder why he's throwing popcorn at some stranger when I see who's sitting in front of her: Nate and Ryan. When will those fags get a clue?

I admit, the popcorn on the woman's head is kind of funny, but I feel embarrassed. "Dude, really?" I say to Josh.

He looks at me, grinning. "What?"

He tries again. This time the popcorn hits Ryan's ear. He twists around. Sees us. His face blanches. He leans into Nate. Says something. Nate turns and looks at us. Then his eyes meet mine. He looks … I don't know. Hurt, I guess. I'm thinking, *Hey, doofus, you knew this could happen.* Yet I have the sudden urge to move to the visitor's bleachers, away from Josh and

Fermio. I cross my arms. Nate turns back around.

The game starts. It's kind of an exciting first inning with lots of hits and great fielding. Josh and Fermio watch the game, eating their popcorn instead of throwing it. Angela Cornish catches a scorching line drive for an out.

"Yo, Angela!" Fermio yells, "You're my hero, baby!"

She doesn't acknowledge him.

I nudge Josh. "He knows she's a lesbian, right?"

"Yeah. But he thinks he's such a stud, he can convert her."

Josh and Fermio are so loud and obnoxious that no one's sitting close to us. I am so not into this today.

As the top half of the first inning ends, I see a guy climbing the steps. He comes down our aisle, heading right for us. He's big, older than us, maybe in his mid-twenties. At first I think he's a teacher or coach I've never met. He's going to tell us to shut up or to get lost.

But he sits next to me and asks in a soft voice, "Are you Brett?"

I say, "Yeah."

He says, "I'm Travis. Nate sent me."

CHAPTER 17

I kind of freeze. This guy, Travis, looks like a college quarterback. But if he's a friend of Nate's, then he's probably gay. What's he doing here?

Josh leans forward, looks over at Travis. I can tell he's curious. Wondering if they can get away with more pranks, or if this guy is going to narc on them. "Hey," Josh says.

"Hey," Travis says, smiling.

Josh straightens. Whispers to me, "Friend of yours?"

I shake my head.

The bottom half of the first inning starts.

Travis leans in a little, says, "Don't worry, I won't talk loud enough for your friends to hear."

"What do you want?"

"I guess it's more about what *you* want. Nate said you were asking him questions."

I don't say a word. What the f———? I look down the stands at Nate. He's focused on the game.

Travis says. "He told me you were asking *for a friend*. But I assume the friend is you." When I still don't respond, he says, "I'm bisexual. Is there anything you'd like to ask me?"

I grip the edge of the bench. My breathing turns shallow. It's like he's diseased. I want him to go away. But I don't. Because, yeah. There is one thing I'd really like to ask. "How do I stop it?"

"You don't. Your feelings for men may change a little, but they'll never go away. Next question."

I gape at him.

"Look," he says, "I'm not trying to be an a-hole. But we don't have much time. Your friends are going to get curious, and I have to get back to work."

I look over at Fermio and Josh. They are focused on rating the bodies of the visiting team's players. "Why are you here?"

"Because I was in your shoes once. I got so depressed about it I almost killed myself. I guess you can say I'm paying it forward." Then he says, "So I'm guessing you like girls. But there's a guy you're crushing on."

I hesitate. "Yeah."

"Same thing happened to me. I was about fourteen. Totally loved girls. Was at the mall one day, thought, 'Wow, that person is hot.' Then I realized it was a guy.

I got very confused. It's been the same ever since. Not the confused part, but the hot-guy part." He pauses. "Are you feeling pretty bad about yourself?"

"Duh. What do you think?"

"Let me give you the upside of being bi. We aren't attracted to people based on their gender. We're flexible. That's pretty cool once you get used to it. On the downside, people will want to tell you you're either gay or straight. Don't let anyone pressure you to make that kind of choice. You are who you are."

"Yeah, right." I hiss through clenched teeth. "What about my friends? My family?"

"Your true friends are going to accept you no matter what. But only tell people you feel comfortable telling. The first person I told was a new girlfriend. I was seventeen. I felt like she had a right to know. And she was fine with it. Now it gets easier every time I come out."

I'm shaking my head. "No," I whisper so low I wonder if he can hear me. "I can't come out. Ever."

"It feels good to tell someone. Believe me. But it's your choice. I'm just sharing my experiences."

"Well, stop sharing!" I hiss. "I don't need your help."

Suddenly everyone's leaping to their feet, cheering. I stand too, not wanting to draw attention to Travis and me. Something touches my hand. He's handing me what looks like a business card. I don't want to take it, but I quickly shove it in my back pocket before anyone notices. He pats my shoulder and leaves. I want to slug him.

Out on the field, a player is leisurely rounding the bases, pumping her fist in the air. She must have hit a home run.

As we sit back down, I see Travis reach the bottom of the bleachers. He walks toward the parking lot.

Josh asks, "Who was that guy? What were you talking about?"

"He's … just some guy. A brother of one of the players."

"Oh yeah? Which player?"

"Um … I don't know."

"He said he was a player's brother but he didn't say who?"

I glare at Josh. "No! He didn't say!"

Josh holds up his hands. "Okay. Chill."

Fermio leans over and stares at me. "What's going on?"

I take a huge breath. Press my hands on my knees. I feel like crying. I just effing want to cry.

Five rows down, Nate turns, looks at me. What? Does he want me to mouth thank you? Thanks for sending your bi friend to remind me how truly horrible my life is. To try and recruit me into your gay club. You faggot. You stupid faggot.

I run my hand through my hair. Jump up. "I have to go," I tell Josh and Fermio.

I hop down off the bleachers. There's the thick metallic *thwang* of a bat hitting a ball. I notice a bat leaning against the end of the dugout. With everyone screaming, their eyes on the field, I grab it. I hold it next to my body as I walk to the parking lot.

I find Nate's car. His stupid gay Civic. I look around the lot. Don't see anyone. I pull the bat up over my right shoulder. Bash it against a headlight. The glass breaks with a satisfying crunch. I smash the other headlight. I raise the bat again. Bring it down on the hood with all of my strength. All of my balled-up anger. I do it again. And again.

I'm panting. Staring at Nate's ruined car. Feel like I can't move. Then I shake myself out of it. Carry the bat to my pickup. Get inside. My heart is beating fast against my ribs. I'm trembling all over. Reaching behind me, I throw the bat behind the seat.

I sit there a second. What did I just do?

Turning the key in the ignition, the engine stutters. On the third try, it starts. I slowly back out of the parking space. I pay attention to the speed limit as I drive away from school. Check the rearview mirror for flashing red and blue lights.

CHAPTER 18

I should go home. Instead, I drive. And keep driving. I've only got a few dollars on me. So I stop when there's just enough gas in the tank to get me home. I park at a county beach. Walk out on the sand. Sit with my back against a dune. It's foggy. The sand and air are cold. The chill seeps through my jeans and thin hoodie. It's like I haven't stopped shivering since I left school. At least the cold gives me something to focus on besides my brain.

I listen to the waves crashing in. The squawking seagulls. Fish trawlers bob like toy boats out on the water. One of them

might be my dad's. It's weird thinking I
might be looking at my dad out there. I
lower my eyes. Grab a piece of driftwood
and draw marks in the damp sand. Mom
used to bring Darla and me here. On Satur-
days when Dad was fishing.

Mom was a loving person. An under-
standing person. I think that's why Dad
kind of fell apart after she died. He misses
her like crazy. I do too. Especially now. I
could walk into the kitchen today, tell her
about me, and I think she'd get it. She'd
love me anyway.

I start drawing circles. Wonder who I
can count on. Who my friends are. Yesterday, I would have said Jillia. I'm not sure
anymore. A week ago, I would have said
Fermio, Josh, the other guys on the team.
Now I'm not sure about them either. How
can I be friends with guys who'd hate me
if they knew who I really was? They might
not throw popcorn at my head or try to

steal my backpack. I'm too big for that. No, they'd find more underhanded ways to get at me. Like what I did to Nate's car. Or worse. I can imagine it getting so bad I might have to quit the football team. Maybe go to a different school. I don't know how Nate and his friends cope.

The breeze picks up. I wrap my arms around my legs and rest my chin on my knees. I laugh to myself. The only person I consider a friend I've known for two weeks. Zach. He's not an arrogant jock. He's just a nice guy. With a good sense of humor. And he likes me. I think the same way I like him. I'm not sure. I'm tired of not being sure.

It's really getting cold. I scramble to my feet and brush off the sand. Hike back to the truck. Catch a glimpse of the bat behind the seat. Feel sick to my stomach. Don't want to think about Nate discovering his bashed-in car. Or wonder if the cops are searching for me. So I push it out of my head.

I drive toward home. But instead of taking my turnoff, I keep going. Drive downtown. Hang a right on Fifth. Park up the street from Coffee Plantation. Sit in the Nissan a minute. Listen to the hot engine *click-click-click* as it cools. I made a promise to myself this morning. That I wouldn't come here. I guess some promises are impossible to keep.

The coffee shop is more crowded than before. All the tables are taken. It's the same people with their laptops and e-readers. Weird, but I don't feel like such an outsider today. I'm not one of them, but I don't feel like I've landed on an alien planet either.

I get in line at the counter. Zach is ringing up another customer. When he sees me, his broad smile just about knocks my socks off.

"Hey, Brett! Mocha? Whipped?"

"Yeah. Thanks."

"Good to see you, man. We're kind of busy. Give me a few minutes until things calm down."

"Cool."

After giving the cashier my last four dollars, I take my paper coffee cup to a small table that someone just left. Glance at the artwork on the walls. Wonder if any of it is Zach's. I sip the drink, trying not to be too obvious as I catch glimpses of him behind the counter. The blue apron he's wearing is lame, but on him it looks good. Shows off his broad shoulders. He must work out. He didn't build up those muscles slinging coffee. I guess I could ask him. He looks over at me while he's waiting for a woman to figure out her order. He smiles and shrugs.

As I smile back, Jillia pops into my head. I'm stabbed by guilt. What if Zach

153

were a girl? Should I be sitting here ogling her? Admiring how she looks in her apron? Well, as long as I don't act on my ogling, what's the harm?

As I take another sip of the mocha, it's obvious what the harm is. I want to do more than admire Zach. I want to know what it's like. To be with a guy. With a guy I'm crazy about. With him. That would make me a cheat. Which means I shouldn't do anything more than what I'm doing right now—looking.

Except I don't know if I can spend the rest of my life pushing away this part of myself. Denying who I am. My cup empty, I crush it in my hand.

"Ready?"

I look up. Zach's dangling a keychain in his raised fist.

"Yeah." I hesitate a second. Then I'm out of my chair.

I follow him out the back door. Into the parking lot. Against the gloomy alley, the Mustang looks like a red cherry on a slab of chocolate ice cream. He unlocks the driver's-side door. Pops the hood.

"This is all a mystery to me, but I thought you might want a look." He raises the hood and props it open. Rests his hands on the front of the engine compartment. I stand next to him. Close enough to feel the heat coming off his arm.

Under the hood, there's chrome everywhere. Chrome valve covers. Chrome air filter. What isn't chrome is black or brushed aluminum.

"I've never seen such a pristine engine in my life," I tell him. "It makes my truck look like a junk heap."

"I guess Sarah and her boyfriend put tons of hours into this. I keep telling her I'm going to draw it."

I laugh and look at him. "Yeah, you would."

He shrugs. "What can I say? I like interesting shapes." He meets my eyes. I remember him drawing me this morning. If I move closer, our lips will touch. I quickly lower my eyes, heat rising to my face.

"Seen enough?" he asks.

I nod.

He lets the hood close with a gentle slam. "Okay, now for the interior. It is so sweet. You're gonna love this."

He sits on the driver's seat. Unlocks the passenger door from the inside. I feel myself standing on a thin edge about to slide. If I'm going to leave, I need to do it now.

Right now.

CHAPTER

19

I look around the empty parking lot. The empty alley. Hear the car window roll down. "You okay?" Zach calls. "Have to babysit your sister again?"

I hesitate. Think how lame it would seem if I ran away again. "No," I answer as I slowly walk over and open the passenger door. Sit on the bucket seat. The upholstery is butter-soft leather, the same red as the exterior. "Wow. This is nice." I can't help rubbing my hands over the seat cushion.

"Right? I told you it was sweet."

I look around the interior. "It's like the car is fresh off the lot. Only better."

"Exactly. Not bad for something older than my parents." He slouches down a little. Holds the steering wheel like he's driving. "Sarah says it was totally rusted and ready for the junkyard when they bought it." He grabs the gearshift in his right hand. "Too bad it's a manual transmission. I'll never get to drive it." He turns his head. "Do you know how to drive a stick?"

I nod. "My Nissan's a five speed."

"Really? Wow, that's old school. I am impressed."

"It's not a big deal. Once you get the hang of it." I point toward his feet. "You just press your left foot down on that far pedal."

"This one?" He taps the clutch with the toe of his sneaker.

"Yep. Go ahead and push it."

When I see his leg extend, I press my hand over his on the gearshift. I do it without thinking. Like when my dad wrapped his arm around me and my fishing pole the first time I cast a line. Zach's warm skin against my palm is incredible. I shouldn't be doing this. It's too weird. But if Zach thinks it's weird, he doesn't flinch.

I swallow. "Push forward," I say, my voice thick. I press our hands up. "That's first." I pull our hands down. "That's second."

Our hands are the same size. Fit perfectly together. I want to lace my fingers through his. Pull his hand against my chest. I'm so close to doing it, I freak. Let go. "Sorry," I mumble. "I guess you don't need me pushing you around."

"That's okay. It helps." He says it calmly. Like guys grab his hand every day. Maybe they do. Then he says, "So there's more than first and second, right?"

"Um … right." I take a deep breath. My hands gripping my knees, I tell him, "Third is up and to the right. Fourth is down and right."

I hear the gearbox clunk into place as he goes through the motions.

"Then back to the middle is neutral."

He grins at me when he's done. "Cool. Though I'm assuming it's not this easy when you're driving."

"Uh, yeah, it's a little more complicated. You can practice on my truck if you like. Sometime. It's an old clunker. You're not going to hurt it too much if you screw up."

"Really? Yeah, I've always wanted to drive a stick. Like only wimps drive automatics, right?"

He smiles. Looks me in the eyes. I've got to stop dancing around this. I've got to say something. Get my feelings out in the open. Find out what his feelings are. "Hey, uh, Zach—"

There's a knock on the driver's-side window. We both jump.

A girl with long black hair is smiling at us through the glass. Zach rolls the window down. "Hey!" he says.

"Hey." She leans in and kisses him on the lips.

Zach says, "Nicole, this is Brett. Brett, Nicole."

She grins. Her eyes brighten. "Oh, the guy from art class! Zach told me about you." She sticks her hand into the car. I shake it. "Nice to meet you."

"Yeah," I mutter. "Same here."

Zach's eyes widen. "Oh no. What time is it?" He opens the door. "Sarah's gonna kill me. I told her I'd only be gone a minute." He jumps out of the car.

I do the same.

Zach waves at me. "See you in class tomorrow?"

"Yeah." I wave back.

"Thanks for the stick-shift lesson."

"Sure. Thanks for the car tour."

I shove my hands in my pockets. Watch as Zach and Nicole wrap their arms around each other and trot back to the coffee shop.

I take a last, lingering look at the Mustang. Make sure the doors are locked, feeling strangely responsible for it. I walk through the alley to the street. Back to my truck. I stick the key in the ignition. Sit there with my hand on the gearshift. Feel tears pressing against my eyes. I go ahead and let them out. Don't give a crap who sees me.

I sit there for a long time. Miserable. Frustrated. So Zach has a girlfriend. I do too. But since he didn't pick up on my awkward pass, I'm ninety-nine percent sure he's not gay or bi. That means romantically, sexually, he's off-limits. It can never go further than friends. I can't believe how sad I feel. And embarrassed that I let it go as far as it did.

I look around for something to wipe my snotty nose with. Have to settle for the semi-clean corner of an oil rag. I don't know what to do. Right now. Ever. I can't imagine going through this again. Falling for a guy. Not knowing if he's gay or straight or whatever. Being afraid to find out. Being afraid of other people finding out about me. I hate this. I hate my lame-ass life!

I look out the window. It's dark. I need to get home. Turning the key in the ignition, I hear a pathetic *click*.

S——t! I slam the steering wheel. Jump out of the truck and look under the hood. The wires are firmly connected. It doesn't surprise me when I try again and the engine doesn't start.

I take a deep breath.

Home is a couple miles away. I could walk. Call Dad for a ride. But he'll ask why I'm parked downtown. I don't feel like answering a bunch of his paranoid questions. I could call my buddies. But they'll ask their own stupid questions, and I can't deal with their macho crap right now. Jillia's house is just a few blocks from town. The game must have ended a while ago. She's probably home. It would be good to see her. Maybe I can try apologizing again.

The more I think about making things right with Jillia, the better I feel. She's my girlfriend. I love her. I really want to see her.

I pull out my phone. See a couple of messages, both from Dad. Asking me where I am. I call and tell him I'm doing homework at Jillia's.

"Why didn't you call back?"

"Sorry. I turned off my phone and lost track of time."

Another pause. Then a gruff, "You know I like being able to reach you. Be home by nine." He hangs up.

I start to call Jillia, then change my mind. Maybe she'll be more receptive if I show up on her doorstep like a lost puppy.

CHAPTER 20

I sink my hands into my hoodie pockets as I walk the five blocks to Jillia's. It's sprinkling and freezing-ass cold. She doesn't have a car, but the one she drives—her mom's minivan—is parked in the driveway.

I take a deep breath before I knock. Man, I hope she's in a good mood. Her mom opens the door a crack.

"Oh. Brett." Her voice is a bit icy. But that's not unusual for her. She narrows her eyes. "Is Jillia expecting you?"

"No. I'm just stopping by. Is she here?"

"Just a minute."

She closes the door in my face. Wow. Couldn't even invite me in? I stamp my feet on the cement porch to stay warm. It feels like I'm out here an hour when Jillia finally comes to the door. She's frowning. Says, "What are you doing here?"

"I'd like to talk to you."

"I told you to leave me alone for a while."

"I know." I shiver. Try to think what to say. How to get past her anger. "Look, my truck stalled. Downtown. The alternator finally conked out. I walked over here. I thought maybe you could give me a ride."

"What about your dad?"

"He's … busy."

She stares at me.

"Do you mind if I come in for a second? I'm freezing my butt off out here."

She sighs. "Yeah. Okay." She opens the door and closes it behind me. "I need to get a jacket and change my shoes."

I start to follow her to her bedroom. She twists around. "Stay here please."

I stop in my tracks. "Okay." I guess we won't be having a heart-to-heart in her bedroom. At least we can talk in the car.

I stand awkwardly near the living room. The rest of her family is watching TV. "Hey," I say with a nod. "How's it going?"

Jillia's dad usually asks me about football or school or something. He just glances at me and nods. Her mom is nervously tapping the armrests of her easy chair. At first I'm thinking that whatever is on TV must be really gripping. Then I think, they hate me. Way more than usual. What did Jillia tell them?

She's back, sweeping through the room. Says to her parents, "I'm giving Brett a ride home. I'll be back in a minute."

Her dad looks up, suddenly concerned. "Are you sure?"

"Yeah."

"Do you have your phone with you?"

"Yes."

Then we're out the door. Once in the van I ask, "Did you tell them we did it or something?"

Her eyes widen. "Are you crazy? Of course not."

"Then what was going on back there? Why do they hate me all of a sudden?"

She shrugs. "I told them I'm breaking up with you."

My stomach tightens. "What?"

She starts the car. "I've been thinking about it a lot lately. Today it was all I thought about. Even during the game." She backs out of the driveway. Puts the van in drive. "It's the only decision that feels right, Brett." She says it so matter-of-factly. So definitively.

I lean my head against the headrest. "I'm sorry," is all I can think to say. I mean it in so many ways that I'll never be able to explain to her.

She says sadly, "Yeah. Me too." Then she says, "You know what kept running through my head all day? Watching you and Fermio pick on Nate and Ryan at practice last week. You guys are bullies. I've always known it. It just never really bothered me until I experienced it firsthand."

My jaw drops. "You're saying I bullied you?"

She doesn't respond.

"Jillia. What are you talking about?"

She glares at me. "Sex, Brett!"

"I bullied you into having sex?"

She stares out the windshield. "Yes."

I think about it. "Okay. Maybe I pressured you a little. But bullied? No way."

"That's how it felt to me."

"Wow. Really?" I start scrambling. "What if I tell you I'm not that person anymore?"

"I would say your timing is pretty convenient."

I want to tell her about Zach. About being bisexual. About what I've been going through these past two weeks. But I can't risk it. She might tell someone, like her parents. Or Shannon. Then it would be all over the school. "It's true, Jillia. I'm not kidding. This isn't some *convenient* excuse. I have changed. For what it's worth, I think we're bullies too. We're total assholes."

She pulls up in front of my house. Leaves the engine running. Looks at me. "For your sake, I hope you have changed. Good-bye, Brett."

I hold her gaze. Try to find the spark that used to be there. Want more than anything to kiss her, start the fire up again. But I guess that would be pressuring. In her eyes, bullying.

I jump out and close the door.

The sound of her van fades down the street as I walk slowly to the back door. The kitchen is empty. The TV is on, one of Dad's shows. I realize I haven't eaten dinner. I open the fridge, more out of habit than hunger. My stomach is churning. I let the door close.

On the way to my bedroom, Dad says, "Call me next time you're going to be late."

He's slouched in his easy chair, staring at the TV. "Why?" I ask. "You don't care."

He glances up. "What's wrong with you?"

"Nothing! Forget it." I storm to my room. Slam the door.

I hate this place! I pace across the floor. Pull at the roots of my hair. In one day I lost my girlfriend. Found out the guy I wanted to be gay isn't. Bashed in Nate's car. No one understands me. I don't understand me either. I don't know what I am. Who I am. I hate this! I hate me!

I sit on my bed. Jump up again. Feel like I've got ants crawling over my skin.

There's a knock at the door. Dad sticks his head in. "What's going on?"

Man, this day just keeps getting better.

Dad walks into my room. Closes the door behind him. "Talk to me, Brett."

"I told you. Nothing is going on."

He stares at me. "How could you say I don't care about you? Of course I care about you."

I throw my hands up. "You won't let me get a job. The alternator on the truck finally went out today. Now I have to come begging to you for cash again. I need gas too."

"Why didn't you say so?" He reaches into his pocket. Pulls out some bills. "I had a good haul yesterday. The alternator is thirty bucks, right?"

"Dad! That's not the point!"

He hands me a couple of twenties and a ten. I don't take them.

"Here!" He shoves the money at my chest.

I back up. "I don't want your money! Don't you get it? I can earn it myself. I can help you, Dad. I can help us. I can even buy Darla a chicken or whatever. We're a family, right?"

He sets the cash on my desk. Scratches the back of his neck. "I don't want you—"

"I know! You don't want me getting stuck in some dead-end job for the rest of my life. I promise I won't."

He shakes his head.

"Dad, I'm not twelve anymore. You don't need to protect me from Mom dying. She's dead. She's gone. Let's move on."

It's like the air in the room has been sucked out. He presses his lips together. His eyes get red and watery. He opens his mouth to say something. Closes it. Sits on my desk chair like someone pushed him down. Rests his head in his hands. I can't tell if he's crying because he's being quiet about it. But I'm pretty sure he is.

Great. I don't know what to do. I can't believe what I just said. But it's true. I'm not going to take it back. I sit on my bed. Wait for him to finish. I can't stand seeing him like this. This has been *such* a crappy day.

He finally looks up. Rubs his eyes with the heels of his palms. Takes a deep breath. "Is the job at Earl's still open?"

"I don't know."

"Let me think about it."

I nod.

He gets up. Hesitates. Stares at me. "There's something else going on, isn't there?"

I shrug my shoulders.

"You can tell me, Brett. You're right. We're a family. Whatever is bothering you, I want to hear it."

I stare at my shoes. Wonder how much to say. "Jillia broke up with me."

He sighs. "I'm sorry. I've been there. It hurts." He rubs his cheek. "Anything I can do?"

"Yeah." I wait a beat. "You can kill me."

I meant it to come out as a joke. But I guess my voice wasn't all that funny.

Dad doesn't laugh. He crosses the room. Sits next to me on the bed. I smell fish. The aftershave he slathers on to cover the fish. "I know it seems like the end of the world. But you're sixteen. You'll have more girlfriends."

It's such a stupid thing to say. I don't want another girlfriend. I want Jillia. This does feel like the end of the world. But he doesn't know how much worse it is. That Jillia is just the tip of the iceberg. I take a deep breath. Start thinking about earlier today. What Travis said about knowing who to trust. That it helps to tell someone. Tell my dad? It never even occurred to me. I'm not sure how he might take it. But I *can* trust him. No matter what I say, I know it won't go any further than this room.

"It's not just Jillia." I glance up at him. "It's. …" I shake my head. I can't. I just can't.

"Brett," he says. "Tell me. Whatever it is, we'll get through it."

I sit there for a long time. He doesn't move. Doesn't say anything. Like he's on his boat, waiting for the fish to show up. Slowly, I start talking. Tell him about art class. My feelings for Zach. Then I go back to summer camp, to Jerry. It's painful. Embarrassing. As I trip over my words, I keep tabs on him. At the slightest sign he's freaking out, I'll stop. Tell him to forget it. It's no big deal. I'll get over it.

But he sits still, listening. Stares at the floor, his hands gripping the edge of the bed. When I'm done, part of me doesn't care about his response. I told someone. It's off my chest. I'm relieved.

Dad clears his throat. Rubs his hands on his thighs. "I'm not sure what to say." He glances at me. "You're pretty certain about all of this?"

I nod.

He reaches out. Rests his hand on my shoulder. "You're my son, Brett. I love you. No matter what. Okay?"

I nod again. Feel tears coming. Push them back. I did enough crying earlier.

"Is there anything I can do for you?" he asks. "Do you want to see someone? A counselor maybe?"

I shake my head. "I just want to live my life, you know? I want to play football.

Have friends. Go to college." I pause. "Fall in love. Maybe have a family."

"Of course." He smiles and says, "Thanks for telling me. I know that must have been hard."

The door slowly opens. Darla sticks her head in. "What are you guys talking about?"

Dad squeezes my shoulder and lets go. "Guy talk," he says. "But I think we're done." He raises an eyebrow at me.

"Yeah. You can come in," I tell her.

She bounds across the floor and leaps between us on the bed. She leans her head on Dad's arm, and he wraps his arm around her. "So, a chicken, huh?"

She winces. "Larissa kept crying when we ate her hen for dinner. I don't think I can handle that."

I smile. Keep myself from saying *I told you so*.

"So I'm thinking about a milking goat."

"A milking goat," Dad repeats. He smiles at me over her head. "We'll see."

I roll my eyes.

Dad gets to his feet. "Come on. Let's let Brett do his homework."

Darla runs out. As Dad's leaving, I whisper, "There's one more thing."

His eyes kind of bug out. Like, what more could there possibly be? But he nods for me to go on.

"It's a long story. But I was super-pissed off this afternoon and bashed a kid's car with a baseball bat. I don't think anyone saw me. But if they did, I might be arrested. If no one saw me, I still need to pay for the damage."

He shakes his head. "Brett."

"I know! It was stupid. I just wanted to let you know. In case you have to bail me out or something."

He closes his eyes a second. Takes a deep breath. Then he reaches out and pats my arm. "Why don't you find out if that job is still open."

"So you're okay with me working?"

"Yes. Just remember your promise. You're not going to stay at Earl's forever."

"Thanks, Dad. I'll remember."

CHAPTER

22

Josh gives me a ride to school the next day. Asks, "So why did you skip out of the game yesterday?"

I shrug. "Remembered something I needed to do."

"Okay." He grins. "Funny. Nate's car got wrecked during the game. The timing is kind of interesting."

"What are you talking about?"

He shrugs. "Whatever, man."

I need to play this out. "What happened to Nate's car?"

"The front was totally bashed in. Like, with a bat. You should have seen Nate crying over his poor car. Puffed out like he was about to explode. Accused us of doing it. It was hysterical. We calmly pointed out we were in the stands the whole game." Josh laughs.

"Wow," I say. "Yeah, I didn't notice."

My stomach knots. When we get to the parking lot, Nate's car isn't there. I wonder if he's at school today. I have to talk to him. It's not a conversation I'm looking forward to. But I can't have this hanging over my head.

At my locker I keep expecting Jillia to sneak up behind me. Tickle my sides. I want to smell her apple hair. Taste her blueberry lips. As I'm shoving books into my locker, I see her walking down the hallway with Shannon and some of her other friends. Jillia doesn't even glance at me. She is so beautiful. My heart breaks all over again. Maybe, after a while, she'll come around.

But then I think about Travis telling his girlfriend about being bi. I don't think I could ever tell Jillia. Partly because I don't think she'd accept it. Partly because I don't trust her to keep it to herself. I agree with Travis. I believe whoever I'm with has the right to know who I am. I guess that means I need to get over Jillia. I slam my locker closed.

Art class. Great. I stand in the doorway. Zach's there. I walk in. Sit next to him like we're friends. Buddies. Because we are. I admit I spend part of the class admiring his broad shoulders. His ripped biceps. I smell his delicious arm when he reaches over to show me how to shade the side of the tree trunk I'm drawing. We also talk and laugh about stuff. Will it be painful keeping my feelings for him locked up? Totally. But it's worth it to keep our friendship. Because I'm not sure what my future looks like. At some point I may need all the friends I can get.

I skip out of class a little early. When I talked to Nate under the bleachers, he said he shared math with a couple of my football buddies. I'm pretty sure which class he was talking about. I wait outside the door. The bell rings. Fermio is the first student out.

"Hey, Miller," he says. We bump forearms. "What's up?"

As normally as I can, I say, "I have to talk to Nate."

He grins. "Gay Nate?"

"Nate. Yeah. About an assignment."

He leans against the wall, still smiling. "This I've got to see."

"It's not a prank, dude."

Nate comes out the door.

"Nate!" I call.

His eyes widen when he sees me and Fermio. He keeps walking.

"Nate! Wait up!"

"What's going on?" Fermio asks.

"Nothing. I'll see you later." I catch up with Nate. Walk next to him. "We need to talk."

He looks over. Slows a little when he sees Fermio isn't with me. "What about?"

"Your car."

He stops in the middle of the hallway. I pull him out of the way before we get trampled. Then I tell him what I did. And why. I apologize. Tell him I'll pay for the damage. Or fix his car myself. His back is rigid the whole time I'm talking.

In the hallway I hear a sing-songy, "Brett and Nate, sitting in a tree! K-i-s-s-i-n-g!" Fermio is walking past us with a couple of the guys. He kisses the back of his hand with a loud SMACK!

I smile at him. Yell, "Screw you!" and flip him off.

Nate's mouth is open. He's holding on to his orange backpack straps like they're lifelines. "Okay," he says. "I won't press charges."

I take a deep breath. "Thanks."

He looks at the floor, then back at me. "Sorry about Travis. I should have asked you first if it was okay."

"Probably." Then I say, "I have to get to English."

"Brett," he says. "We're having a GSA meeting on Wednesday—"

"No!" I glare at him. "Look, Nate. I won't harass you anymore. And I'll try my best to keep my friends from harassing you. But that's it. I'm not *open*, okay? And I expect you to keep what we talked about to yourself."

He nods quickly. "Okay. Yeah. Of course."

Saturday, I'm standing at the back gate at Earl's. It's 7:20 a.m., ten minutes before my shift starts. Earl's not here yet.

I hear keys jangle behind me. Turn around.

Earl is grinning. "Wow," he says. "Eager beaver. I like it."

I shrug, feeling a little dorky. My first day at my first real job. "I couldn't sleep," I admit.

He unlocks the gate. Lets me in. "Did that alternator work?"

"Yeah. Great." On Wednesday Dad drove me to Earl's, then to Fifth Street. He helped me change out the alternator. "Thanks for the discount."

"No problem. Other than your measly pay, that's your only perk. Take advantage of it."

Once we're in the store, he claps his hands. "Okay. Task number one. Make coffee."

The morning goes by fast. I don't know what I'm doing half the time. But Earl is patient. Mostly he sends me out to the yard to find parts and tear them out. That's fine. It's my favorite job anyway.

During my lunch break, a sandwich in one hand, I'm out in the yard again. Searching. I find what I'm looking for—a Honda Civic. It must have been rear-ended. The back is a mess but the hood is in good shape. I think it's the right year. I'll have to check with Nate.

Across from the Civic is a yellow Mustang. I shake my head at the coincidence and lean on the hood. Eat my sandwich. When I'm done with lunch, I pull out my phone. Reach in my back pocket. Pull out the business card that's still there. Travis scribbled his cell number on the back. Taking a deep breath, I punch in the numbers. Think about what I want to say, what I want from him.

I guess what I'm mostly looking for is someone who understands. Friendship, maybe. And courage, I guess. Because one of these days there will be another Zach. And he won't be straight. And I won't be in another relationship. And then. ...

Then I'll have to see how brave I am.

I press the Call button.